The Painted Tent

VICTOR CANNING

The Painted Tent

William Morrow & Company, Inc.
New York 1974

For Jack and Molly

Contents

↶ *The Duchess Takes a Look Ahead* ↷

Smiler surfaced slowly from a deep and dream-filled sleep. In the few moments before he opened his eyes Smiler had no idea where he was or what had happened to him. His arms and legs ached; there was a crick in his back, and a heavy weight on his lap.

He opened his eyes. Resting on his lap was a large Siamese cat with a torn left ear. Smiler found that he was sitting in the front of a small car. Through the windscreen he could see the slope of a heather-covered hill and a clump of red-berried rowan trees. Beside the road ran a small stream, swirling and cascading over sun-bathed grey boulders and flanked by tall bracken growths. A pair of hooded crows flew out of the trees and a yellow wagtail dipped and bowed on one of the stream boulders.

A shadow fell across the window at his side and a man's voice said cheerfully, "Wakey-wakey! Go dip your face in the burn, lad, and then there's a mug of coffee waiting."

Standing by the door was a large-faced, middle-aged man wearing a battered straw boater with a coloured ribbon around it. He had a black, thickly waxed sergeant-major's moustache that curled into sharp points at each end. His dark eyes held a lazy, good-humoured twinkle.

Memory coming slowly back to him, Smiler said politely, "Good morning, Mr. Jago."

"And a good morning to you, Samuel Miles." The man lifted the cat – which Smiler now remembered was called Scampi – from his lap, and went on, "Down to the burn with you."

Stiffly Smiler made his way to the stream, splashed water over his head and face, and then wiped himself on his handkerchief. The water was ice-cold. It brought the colour back to his cheeks, and drove away the fuzziness of the uncomfortable night. He realized now that he must have slept while Mr. Jago went on driving through the night. Mr. Jago, he thought, looked as fresh as a daisy. And Mr. Jimmy Jago, Smiler acknowledged, had been good to him for he had picked him up late on the Fort William road and had helped him to get well away from trouble.

Going back to the car Smiler said to himself – for Smiler was a great one for talking to himself in times of trouble or doubt – "You were lucky, Samuel M., that Mr. Jago came along." Although most people called him Smiler he didn't himself much care for the name. He preferred Samuel Miles, or better still, Samuel M., which was what his father called him. At the thought of his father a shadow passed across Smiler's thoughts.

At the back of the car, which was a very old four-seater tourer, were set out three small wooden boxes. On one of them was a camping-stove, roaring gently to itself while a saucepan of coffee simmered on top of it.

Mr. Jago, opening a tin of sardines for Scampi, looked up and said, "Sit yourself down, lad, and take some coffee. No food for us – we'll get breakfast later. But animals is different. If Scampi don't get his regularly, then he'll howl his head off until he does."

Smiler sat on his box, cradling a mug of hot coffee in his hands, and Mr. Jago sat on his box with his mug. Scampi crouched on the grass and ate his sardines from a small saucer. Scampi was far too great an aristocrat to eat anything straight from the can.

Mr. Jago sat there, eyeing Smiler, and saw nothing to turn him from an opinion he had formed very soon after he had picked him up the previous night. The lad was in trouble and, more than that, the lad was down in the dumps. Jimmy Jago had no difficulty in recognizing this because he had often been in trouble himself – though not so often down in the dumps. He was a good-looking, healthy, strong boy – somewhere around sixteen years old, Jimmy guessed. Yes, a likely-looking lad, tallish, fair-haired, well-built, with a friendly, heavily freckled, squarish face, and he had a pair of angelic blue eyes which, when he smiled, made him look as though butter wouldn't melt in his mouth. Not that he, Mr. Jago, was going to be fooled by that. Boys were boys and trouble clung to them like their shadows – and so it should be because that was what in the end made men of them, good, bad or indifferent.

Mr. Jago finished his coffee and, while Smiler was having a second mug, he lit his battered old pipe, tipped his boater back on his head and, giving Smiler a solemn look, suddenly offset by a slow wink, said, "Right, lad – catechism time."

Smiler, puzzled, said, "Catechism time?"

Mr. Jago grinned. "I was well educated, though there's times when I prefer it not to be obvious. Catechism, from the verb to catechise; meaning to instruct or inform by question and answer. I ask the questions – and you answer 'em if you're in the mood. As the Duchess would say, 'Trouble shared is trouble spared.'"

"Who's the Duchess, sir?"

"We'll come to her later – if necessary. All right, then – catechism. You for it or against it?"

"Well, I . . . I don't know, sir."

"Let's try it then. Full name?"

"Samuel Miles, sir."

"Ever used any others?"

Smiler hesitated. Because he liked the man and was grateful to him and was naturally truthful anyway, unless it was vital to be otherwise, he said, "Now and again, sir."

"A fair answer. Would have had to say the same myself. Right, then – age? And don't keep calling me *sir*."

"Sixteen in October."

"Well, that's only a few days off. Place of birth?"

"Bristol."

"A noble city. Almost as good as Plymouth."

Smiler grinned. "Is that where you were born?"

"Thereabouts – so I'm told. But right or wrong,

4

I'm a real Devon man." As he spoke, his voice was suddenly rich and ripe with a West-Country accent. He went on, "Parents?"

Smiler's face clouded. Slowly he said, "My mother's dead, sir. A long time ago."

"I see. And your father?" Mr. Jago saw Smiler's lips tighten and tremble a little, and with rare understanding said quietly, "Well, we can leave that one for now. Got any relations in Bristol still?"

Smiler said, "Oh, yes. My sister Ethel. She's married to Albert – he's an electrical engineer and plumber. But I don't want to go back to them. Not yet, anyway."

"Nobody suggested it, lad. Now then – what put you on the road, all your gear in a rucksack, flagging me down at nine o'clock of night on a lonely Highland road? Trouble, eh?"

"Yes, sir."

"Police or personal?"

"Well, a bit of both, really. But I'd rather not——"

"Of course. We'll skip it, but keep our eyes skinned for the police." Mr. Jago grinned. "Splendid body of men, as I should know from long experience. How are you fixed financially?"

"I'm all right. I was working and made some money."

"Like work?"

"Of course. If it's the right kind."

"Fair answer. Well then – that about clears it up. No need for the jury to retire to consider a verdict. It's as plain as the freckled nose on your face that you're a case for the Duchess, so we'd better make tracks for her. Take us a couple of days. Maybe a bit more."

"Who's the Duchess, sir?"

Mr. Jago leaned back and blew a cloud of smoke into the sunlit air. A big smile creased his face as he twirled one end of his fine moustache. "The Duchess, my lad? Well, now . . . how would I describe her? She's God's gift to anything in trouble. She's directly descended from Mother Ceres. She's got green fingers that could make a pencil sprout leaves if she put it in the ground. She can talk the human language and a lot of others. She's an angel – though she'd need a thirty-foot wing-span to lift her off the ground. She knows the past and the future and has a rare understanding of the present – and she's got a temper like a force nine gale if you get on the wrong side of her!"

"Crikeys!"

"Exactly, Samuel. Exactly. And she's what you need to straighten out whatever it is that's bothering you. So let's get going."

As Mr. Jago rose and began to pack up the car Smiler said, "Is she really a duchess?"

Mr. Jago nodded. "She is indeed, lad. The only one of her kind, but not the sort you're thinking of because, if she were, then, I suppose, I would be Lord Jimmy Jago – seeing that I'm her son."

*　　*　　*

So, in the company of Jimmy Jago and Scampi, Smiler began the long journey southwards down the length of the country. Sometimes they kept to

6

the main roads and sometimes, when Jimmy obeyed some instinct peculiar to him, they worked their way along side lanes and made detours around the big cities. Sometimes they ate in small cafés or at pull-ups for truck drivers. Sometimes they bought their food and ate under the open sky at the edge of field or wood, and always they slept out with Smiler on the front seat and Jimmy – because of his greater size – in the back, and Scampi – who liked the warmth of a human body – sometimes slept with one or with the other.

As they went Smiler became more and more resigned to his parting from the good friends he had made in Scotland and the little world he had known there.* But never for long could he forget his worry about his father, or still the natural fear he had that the police might find him and send him back to the approved school from which he had originally escaped – and to which he meant never to return if he could avoid it because he had been sent there in the first place for something he had never done.

Jimmy was amusing company but, for all their chat and the stories Jimmy told as they travelled the roads in the ancient car, Smiler never came to know much about Jimmy himself. And he was far too polite to ask any direct questions. Jimmy suffered from no such inhibitions and during their journey he came to know a lot about Smiler – and guessed much more. It was the result of Jimmy's gleanings that brought a surprise for Smiler on the morning of their third day of travel. He was

* See *Flight of the Grey Goose*.

7

fast asleep in the passenger seat when he was awakened by the car being brought to a stop. Smiler saw that they were parked in a street of small neat suburban villas. Smiler recognized at once where he was. It was a Bristol street only a little way from the one in which his sister Ethel and her husband Albert lived.

As he stared puzzled at Jimmy he was greeted by one of the man's slow winks.

"That's right, lad. Bristol. I don't aim to have any near and dear ones worrying about what might have happened to you. Nip along and tell 'em you're all right and not to worry. I'll be waiting."

Five minutes later Smiler eased open the door of Albert's workshop at the back of the house in which he had always lived while his father was away at sea.

Albert looked round from his bench where he was turning a thread on a piece of piping and stared at Smiler. Then slowly he smiled broadly, nodded his head, and said, "Now, ain't that odd? I was only just thinkin' about you."

Smiler, who knew he was all right with Albert, that Albert was always on his side, said, "Where's Sister Ethel?"

"Don't worry about her. She's off to the super-market. Just gone."

Though he was very fond of his sister, Smiler had always been in her bad books, chiefly because – no matter how hard he tried not to – he messed up her neat little house and, according to her, was going to the dogs with the bad company he kept.

Sister Ethel had a natural instinct for magnifying and exaggerating the smallest upset into a mountain of trouble and tragedy.

Smiler said, "That's all right then. But I haven't come back for good, Albert."

"Fair enough, Sammy, fair enough. Just a friendly call to say everything's all right, eh? You chose the right day. The police was here yesterday this time. But I'll have to tell Ethel about this . . . maybe this evening over supper cocoa. You all right for money and everything?"

"Yes, thanks. I worked in Scotland and had some good friends, and there's another waiting. He's going to fix me up . . ." Slowly Smiler's lower lip began to tremble and then he burst out, "Oh, Albert . . . did you . . . did you hear about Dad?"

"That I did. Police told us. Missed his boat in Montevideo and no sign of him since. But that ain't worryin' you, is it? Because if it is – don't let it. I've known your Dad since before you was born. Not the first time he's missed his ship. Not the first time he's disappeared into the blue. But he always turns up."

"But something bad could have happened to him, Albert."

"Think so? Not me. Nor should you. You're just like him. Your sister might worry about you, for instance, when you took off into the blue from that approved school. But did I? No. Like father, like son, I said. Never lost a wink of sleep. That's how you want to look at it, Sammy. Two of a kind, you are. Always land on your feet."

9

What Albert said suddenly struck Smiler as sensible. He hadn't thought about it that way before. Convinced of his own innocence he had run off from the approved school, kept out of the way of the police, found jobs, had adventures and made many friends – and had always been sure that in the end things would turn out right. Particularly the moment when his father got back to help him. *But – all the time people were worrying about him like he was worrying now about his father when there was no reason to worry.*

Albert grinned. "Sinks home, don't it? So, don't worry about your Dad. When you least expect it, he'll turn up. Always did, always will. When you least expect him he'll come marchin' in through the door, breezy as a west wind."

"You really believe that?"

"Yes. And if I was a bettin' man – which I was until I married your sister – I'd bet on it. Still, there's one thing – wherever you fetch up, just now and then drop us a line. Not to the house. Just to me care of the General Post Office, Bristol. I'd just like to be able to give a bit of news to Ethel now and then. Like that – if the police come askin' again, which they will, I can say truthfully, 'No, we ain't had no letter from him here.' Strict truth." He winked.

So Smiler promised that he would write sometimes, and then he left well before his sister was likely to be back.

In the car again with Jimmy, he slowly began to feel much happier. "Samuel M.," he told himself, "you've been making mountains out of molehills. Leave Scotland you had to because of the police. But worryin' about Dad . . . well, Albert's right. All seamen miss their boats now and then. Always fall on their feet, though. Like a cat with nine lives."

Scampi sitting on his lap purred as though he understood and approved.

*　　*　　*

From Bristol they went down through Somerset, taking their time and keeping to the side roads. In the mildness of early October, the light of the declining sun cast a pale golden wash over the country. They climbed the Quantocks and then on to the high stretches of Exmoor with the silver spread of the sea away to their right. They went down into small river valleys, through the white- and pink-washed huddles of old villages, and now and again far away to their left they got glimpses of the high tors of distant Dartmoor.

Jimmy, back in his own West Country, took great gulps of the mild, clear air, sucking it in as though he had been a fish out of water too long. And because he was a well-read, self-educated man and had no reason to disguise the fact at this moment, he told Smiler – who had an appetite for information and knowledge as big as any he ever carried to a well-filled table – many things about his land. He told him of the Monmouth Rebellion on the Somerset marshes, and the merciless Judge Jeffreys who had brought death and exile to the rebels; of the story of *Lorna Doone* and the wild Carver family who had terrorized the countryside; of *Westward Ho!* and Amyas Leigh; of real people like the great Drake; of Frobisher, Raleigh and of the sturdy, dour Cornish miners and their support for Bishop Trelawney. And Jimmy taught Smiler – who had a naturally good voice – songs about them, songs new and old . . . *Judge Jeffreys was a wicked man, he sent my father to Van Diemens land. . . . And shall Trelawney die? Then forty thousand Cornishmen shall know the reason why. . . . There was a little man come from the West, he married a wife she was not of the best. . . .*

For Smiler, it was almost as though he were with his father, for they were both great ones for singing together. Because of this and also of what Albert had said, Smiler felt happier than he had done for a long time (although it was only a few days) and his troubles lifted because in the young there is a natural good balance of the emotions, and dark thoughts like stones sink from sight in the sparkling pool of the present.

But there was one moment when Smiler realized that Mr. Jimmy Jago had his dark troubles, too. Once he stopped where they could get a good view of distant Dartmoor. When Smiler said that he would like to go there some day Jimmy, without looking at him, said in an almost angry voice, "Aye, lad, it's a wild, beautiful place – but there's many there now who could wish they'd never seen it, could wish they were a million miles away from it."

Smiler knew at once what he meant.

He said, "You mean the people in prison there? In Princetown prison?"

Jimmy turned and looked at him and said, "What else would I mean?"

When they drove on it was some time before Jimmy's good spirits came back. But back they did come. An hour later they dropped down into the valley of the River Taw, which had its source high up on distant Dartmoor and flowed to the sea at Barnstaple and out into the wide estuary to meet its sister river the Torridge.

They crossed the river by an ancient stone bridge and then the road began to twist and climb along the sides of a small valley through which ran a wide brook. The sides of the valley were patched with woodland and stubble fields and, high over a plantation of firs, Smiler saw three buzzards wheeling and soaring.

They climbed away from the valley, lost sight of it, and then came back to it down a steep hill. At the bottom of the hill was a long, low farm-house, slate-roofed, with white-washed stone walls. To one side of it were stables, two large stone barns and, beyond them, green meadows and patches of woodland flanking the sides of the twisting brook.

Mr. Jago drove through the open farm gate into the wide gravel space before the house. As the car was pulled up Scampi jumped from Smiler's lap through the open car-door window and disappeared around the corner of the house.

Jimmy Jago grinned. "He's off to see his missus. Travellin' man is Scampi but he's always glad to get back."

As Smiler and Jimmy got out of the car the front door of the farm opened and a woman stepped out into the wide porchway. She was a tall, very plump woman of middle age. She came out to greet them like a galleon under full sail, moving for all her bulk as though her feet only just touched the ground. Her hair was red, a tight mop of close curls, and she wore dangling earrings made from silver coins. The ample folds of her long green dress flapped in the valley breeze. All over the dress was a close design of birds, animals, flowers, signs of the zodiac and other symbols. (During all the time Smiler was to be at the farm he was always discovering some new symbol or bird or animal on the dress. In fact, he sometimes had the feeling that the whole design changed every time she wore it.) Her plump face was jolly and creased with a smile and she had soft brown eyes dark as the waters of a woodland pool.

She cried, "Jimmy!" The next moment she had clamped her arms around him and – though he was a big man – it seemed to Smiler that he momentarily disappeared into the green, multi-patterned folds of her dress. She smacked two great kisses on his face and then released him.

Jimmy stepped back, straightened his boater, and said, "Surprised to see me, Ma?"

"And why should I be? The news was on the wind an hour ago. Yin got it first." Her voice like herself was large and jolly.

"Yin," said Jimmy to Smiler, "is Scampi's wife. And this lady, Sammy, is my mother." Then to his mother he said, "Meet Samuel Miles, Ma. He's

a friend of mine." Then to Smiler he said, "Sammy
– the Duchess."

Smiler held out his hand to the Duchess and
said, "I'm very pleased to meet you, ma'am."

The Duchess took his hand, shook it warmly
and vigorously and said, "Welcome to Bullaybrook Farm, boy." Then cocking her head to one
side she eyed him closely and enquired, "Libra?
Am I right?"

Smiler, puzzled, said, "Please, ma'am?"

"Your zodiac sign," said Jimmy. "When were
you born?"

"October the tenth."

"Then it is Libra," declared the Duchess. "And
this is a good day for you, boy. Yes, a good day.
Mercury's not bothering your sign."

"I brought him along, Ma," said Jimmy,
"because he's in trouble. Thought you could sort
him out a bit – meantime he's got broad shoulders
and good hands so he could be useful around the
place."

"Why not? But remember, boy, for the next
three days always go out of the house right foot first
and come in left foot first." She gave him a wink
and continued, "Come on then – into the house."

She turned and sailed before them and Smiler
was careful – even though he felt that it was really
a joke – to step over the threshold with his left
foot first.

*   *   *

That night Smiler lay awake in bed for a long time
sorting things out. He had been given a small

15

room at the back of the house which looked across to the brook. There were four bedrooms and a bathroom on the first floor. Down below as you came through the porch door was a large hall, to one side of which was a dining-room and then a long farm kitchen, stone-flagged. On the other side was a large sitting-room with an open stone fireplace, the ceiling dark-raftered with oak beams. From there, now, Smiler could just catch the faint mumble of the voices of Jimmy and the Duchess as they talked. A picture of the room was clear in his mind.

Before the fire were a sofa and chintz-covered armchairs. A wide, circular table stood in the middle of the room and there was a big grandfather clock just inside the door. But what had interested Smiler most were the walls of the room. They were covered from floor to ceiling with pictures, framed photographs and old posters and prints, and every one of them had something to do with circuses or fairs. There were photographs of liberty horses, of tiger and lion acts, of performing elephants and seals, of high-wire and trampoline artistes, and trained dogs and pigeons. Some of the photographs were old and faded and some were quite new. The posters were past and present advertisements for travelling circuses, bold, garish colours flaming in the mellow light of the room. Over the fireplace itself was a large oil-painting showing the head and shoulders of a clown with a bulbous red nose, his face masked with traditional makeup, and on his head a battered old tophat. Even under the make-up a half-sad, half-comic expression showed through from the real man. At the foot of the picture was a little gold plaque with the words *The Duke* printed on it in black.

Smiler guessed – and later learned – that the Duke had been the Duchess's husband. A lot of things had become clear to Smiler before he went to bed. While they were having tea in front of the fire Scampi had come into the room followed by another Siamese cat. The two had settled on the hearth and the other cat had started to groom Scampi. The other cat was Yin, Scampi's wife, who was showing her pleasure at having him back from his travels with Jimmy.

Later, while the Duchess was getting the supper, Jimmy had taken Smiler up to his room and explained to him that the Duke had been dead for five years. The Duchess, who had travelled the circuses as a fortune teller, had retired to this farm where – apart from the normal farm work – she took care of a few retired or sick circus animals and boarded others when some circus acts were off the road. Her busiest time, Jimmy said, was just after Christmas when most circus acts took a rest before starting the Spring travels. At the moment there were very few animal boarders at the farm.

Jimmy said, "After you've had a chat with the Duchess tomorrow and if you want to stay and like animals there's a job here until you get yourself sorted out. And – " a distant look came into his eyes – "sorting things out sometimes takes a long time, as you'll learn as you grow older.

Now, unpack your gear, and then you can take a stroll round the place before supper. There's over a hundred acres, mostly wood and hill pasture and over a mile of the Bullay brook. But don't go poking into any of the barns yet or the Ancients will take against you."

"The Ancients?"

"You'll meet 'em. I wouldn't spoil your pleasure."

Lying in bed now, seeing through his window the October sky stippled with bright stars, Smiler remembered how, coming back from his stroll around the brook meadows, he had walked into the farm kitchen and had found the Duchess and Jimmy talking to one another. But it was in a language that meant nothing to Smiler – though later he learned that it was Romany, for the Jago family were of true gypsy descent. Just for a moment, before they saw him, he had the feeling that an argument was going on between the two. The impression had been brief but the memory lingered with Smiler. He wondered now if the Duchess and Jimmy had their troubles just as he had.

Outside a little owl called to its mate and the sound of the brook over its stony bed came in a ceaseless murmur. Smiler began to drift off into sleep and, as he did so, he had a feeling of loneliness which could not be fought down. Behind him in Scotland he had left all his friends . . . the face of Laura, his girl friend, floated before him, cheeks sun-tanned, dark hair lifting in the loch breeze and her deep brown eyes alive with laughter.

How long would it be before he saw her again, how long before he could get out of trouble and do all the things he longed to do? And then his father . . . He sniffed, then tightened his lips against the misery that threatened to claim him. Five minutes later, when the little owl called again, Smiler was deep in sleep.

*   *   *

The next morning Smiler had breakfast in the farm kitchen. He had porridge, two fried eggs and four rashers of bacon, three slices of toast and marmalade, and a large mug of milky coffee, all of which he polished off with ease.

The Duchess nodded approvingly and said, "That's the way I like to see a boy eat. Some folk treat their food as though it was going to bite them. Now then, come along with me and we'll get you settled."

She led the way out of the back door and across a yard to a little walled garden which lay behind one of the barns. There was a small green lawn in its centre and flower-beds all around. Standing on the lawn, almost covering it, was a tent. But it was no ordinary tent. Its shape reminded Smiler of illustrations he had seen in history books of the battlefield pavilions knights in armour had used. It was supported at its four corners by stout poles and its roof was domed, the canvas stretched over a cane framework. From a tall spiked flagpole on the top of the dome a red and white silk pennant flapped in the morning breeze. The tent canvas was striped in red, yellow and blue and over the half-open door was a wooden signboard inscribed:

THE DUCHESS OF MINTORO – THE FUTURE AN OPEN BOOK
Patronised by Royalty

Seeing the look in Smiler's eyes, the Duchess said, "Beautiful, isn't it? I've spent more than half my life working in it. But not since the Duke died. Except for the odd friend now and then. Stands there all through the good weather."

She went into the tent and Smiler, a bit nervous, followed her. She sat down at a cloth-covered table and nodded to him to sit opposite her. She draped a small silk scarf over her red curls and said, "Give me your hands, boy."

Smiler held out his hands and the Duchess took first the left one and then the right one and studied their palms and after a while said, "Young hands, young heart and the future only just beginning to write itself there. But the lines are good, the signs are right. You'll have your share of troubles and your share of happiness. At your age – even though I could tell you more – there's no need to know more. But this I'll tell you – you'll never work inside four walls, but you'll work with your hands and your head in a way no countryman or farmer does."

"I want to be a vet.," said Smiler.

"Maybe. Wanting comes before doing and the future is first shaped by the past and the present and then tidied up and fixed by the Great One."

The Duchess released his hands and after a smile and a chuckle added, "And I'm glad to see you keep your nails clean, boy. That's a good sign. Hands are the tools God gave us. We must respect His gift always. Now then, let's get down to the present troubles and see what we can see."

The Duchess reached out to a sidetable and lifted from it a small stand on which stood a crystal ball. It was covered by a silk cloth which she took off. She made Smiler put the palms of his hands about it for a few moments. Then she signalled to him to take his hands away, gave the crystal a quick wipe with the silk and began to stare in it, saying, "Keep quiet. Don't interrupt, and shut your eyes."

Obediently Smiler shut his eyes. Although he was not quite sure in his mind whether he really believed that the Duchess could read the future and the past, he decided that it would be bad manners to decide that she couldn't. So, he began to think about Laura in Scotland, and his father who had missed his ship at Montevideo, and about the day which seemed so long ago now when all his troubles had begun back in Bristol, of the afternoon when an old lady had been jostled off the pavement by a fair-haired boy and her handbag stolen. A policeman seeing the act had gone after the thief. Rounding a corner he had spotted the boy running down the pavement and had finally caught him, still holding the handbag.

The boy had been Smiler, but it was not Smiler who had taken the bag. He had been standing round the corner when a boy he knew – with fair hair like himself, one Johnny Pickering, and no friend of his – came rushing past him and had tossed him the handbag, shouting "Hide it!" Smiler had been caught running away because he was running after Johnny Pickering to make him take the handbag back. But in the juvenile court the parents of Johnny Pickering had sworn that their son had been at home all afternoon and that Samuel Miles was lying to save himself. Smiler had been sent to an approved school but had quickly run away, determined to keep his freedom until his father came back on his boat, the *Kentucky Master*, and could sort things out for him. But Smiler's father had failed to rejoin his boat at Montevideo and the police in Scotland had caught up with Smiler. He had had to go on the run again which was when he had met Jimmy Jago. . . .

Smiler heard the Duchess's voice coming to him, a dreamy far-away voice cutting into his thoughts.

"I see water . . . nothing but water. No . . . now there's a boat. A small boat and a girl in it. She's brown-haired and holding – drat, the boat's gone. . . . Now then, what's this? More water and another boat. But a big one this time and there's a lot of men all lying around in the sun on the deck and one of them's got something. . . . Oh, yes – it's a mouth organ, and he's playing to them———"

Smiler opened his eyes and said quickly, "That's my father. He plays the mouth organ. Is he all right?"

The Duchess said nothing; she just stared at the crystal ball. Her dark brown eyes were fixed as though she were hypnotised, and her big, jolly face was slack and expressionless.

Conscious that he had disobeyed her orders, Smiler closed his eyes and kept silent. After a moment or two the Duchess began to speak again and her voice, now sounding far, far away, gave Smiler an eerie feeling.

". . . Everything's whirling, like coloured snow-flakes . . . Birds, animals, people . . . Ah, there's a room, a big room, the ceiling so high it's lost in shadows, and a grand stairway . . . and oil paintings of fine ladies and noble gentlemen . . . and suits of armour. There are people there, and holly and mistletoe hanging. . . . The girl is there, and the man on the boat, and another man, tall and white-haired and bearded . . . And, yes, yes – you're there Samuel Miles . . . You're all together and there's happiness around you – Oh, no!" The Duchess's voice suddenly broke off. Then, her voice quite different, she went on, "Blood . . . Oh, I don't want to see . . . suddenly such darkness over the bright morning sun . . . and there's a man running . . . running . . . running for his . . .No, no, I don't want to see it."

The Duchess gave a sudden groan and stopped speaking. Smiler, scared, opened his eyes. The Duchess was leaning back in her chair, her hands over her eyes, her shoulders shaking.

Not knowing what to do, Smiler reached out and touched her and said, "Are you all right, ma'am?"

The Duchess dropped her hands from her face, gave herself a little shake, and then suddenly smiled.

23

"I'm all right, boy. There's nothing to worry about. Sometimes the ball goes wild and mixes up the futures. You know the girl and the tall man with the beard?"

"Yes, ma'am."

"And the man with the mouth organ?"

"That's my father."

"Then you need have no worry. Time is going to bring you all together. Whatever happens between now and then, there's that happiness waiting for you."

Smiler considered this and, although he certainly hoped it was going to be true, he didn't see how anyone could ever really see into the future. He said, "You really know that from the crystal ball, ma'am?"

"Of course, boy."

"But . . . well . . . can there be a magic like that? I mean——"

"I know what you mean, boy. You can't understand how anyone can believe in magic?"

"Well, only in a sort of a way, ma'am."

The Duchess smiled. "Then you want to open your eyes, Samuel Miles, and see the magic right under everyone's noses every day of life. You live on a great ball called the earth that spins through space like a top and nobody falls off – that's magic. The sun rises and sets each day, and the seasons come and go – that's all magic. The swallows fly to Africa for the winter and then back here in the Spring – that's magic. But the greatest magic is life itself. The fact that you and every other living thing is alive is the greatest magic of

24

all. Nobody knows how or when it happened except the Great One. What's more, if we can remember the past and live the present, what's so odd about some of us being able to look into the future? It's just a gift, like other people can make music, write poetry, or invent machines that take others to the moon. Magic, Samuel Miles. Every breath we take is part of magic. And my magic is to be able to see a little farther ahead than most other people, and so far as you are concerned you've been told that one day you, your father, that girl, and the tall white-haired man will all be together. Does that chase your worries away?"

"Yes, ma'am, it does. But . . . well, what about the man that was running?"

The Duchess gave Smiler a steady look and then said evenly, "You don't have to worry about him. Just for a moment his future got crossed with yours. Just as telephone calls get mixed up sometimes."

The Duchess took the silk cloth and draped it over the crystal ball. With a warm smile she said, "Right, Samuel Miles – now I want to hear all about yourself and your troubles. Take your time and start from the beginning."

So Smiler told her everything about himself and of all his troubles; starting from the time when Johnny Pickering had come running around the corner and tossed the old lady's handbag to him, through all his adventures since he had run away from the approved school, right up to the moment that Jimmy Jago had picked him up on the road in Scotland.

When he had finished the Duchess said, "Well, you aren't the first that's come to this house with the police after them. Circus and Romany folk sometimes have to follow their own laws – and the police don't like that. But if you keep your fingers crossed and your eyes open you should have no trouble here. The local policeman is a friend of ours. You'd like to stay here, would you?"

"Yes, please, ma'am."

"Well, the wages are small, the work hard, and the food good. And since, if you're going to begin something, there's no time like the present I'll take you over to the Ancients because you'll be working under them."

A bit diffidently, Smiler asked, "Who are the Ancients, ma'am? Are they men?"

"Of course they are."

"And are they very old?"

The Duchess chuckled, her fat chins bobbing and her curls shaking. "They're both old – that's why they're called the Ancients. Bill and Bob Old. That's their name. And a word of warning – never play cards with them for money."

2

∽ *The Starlight Men* ∽

The Duchess took Smiler across the yard to one of the stone barns where he met Bob and Bill Old. They were twin brothers in their early fifties, small, sturdy-looking men with weather-brown, wrinkled faces, bright, mischievous-looking eyes and the perky, cheeky air of a couple of jackdaws. So far as Smiler could see, there was no way of telling them apart except by the clothes they wore. Above his gum boots and corduroy trousers Bob wore a green sweater and on his head, cocked saucily over his iron-grey hair, was a green woollen bonnet with a white bob on the top. Bill's dress was the same, except that his sweater and bonnet were red. But after a few days Smiler realized that the clothes were no sure guide because they swopped clothes some days according to their fancy. They lived a bachelor life in a small cottage up the hill from the farm. Smiler never learned where they had come from or what they had done before they began to work for the Duchess, except that he could guess from their talk that they had both been travelling men and knew a great deal about circuses, fairs and gypsy life. This last he knew because when they didn't want him to know what they were saying they would talk in the Romany language that the Duchess and Jimmy sometimes used.

The Duchess said to them, "Samuel Miles – your new hand. He's a good lad; work him hard, and treat him fair. He's been in a spot of trouble, still is – so he's one of our kind." Then with a look at Smiler, she nodded at the men in turn, saying, "That's Bob – and that's Bill. At least, I think it is." With a chuckle she ruffled Smiler's hair and swept regally out of the barn.

The two men looked at one another and then at Smiler. Then they walked slowly round him and, as they did so, Bill said, "Good shoulders."

Bob said, "Stands well."

Bill said, "Wind sound, I should think."

Bob said, "Let's see how he moves."

Bill said to Smiler, "Trot."

Smiler said, "Please?"

Bob said, "Trot. Once round the barn."

Suspecting that he was having his leg pulled Smiler gave a grin and solemnly trotted round the confined space of the barn.

Bill said, "Nice action."

Bob said, "Sprinter?"

Bill shook his head. "No, stayer."

Bob said, "He'll do then."

Bill said, "Welcome, Samuel Miles."

"Thank you," said Smiler.

Bob said, "You like playing cards?"

Smiler grinned, "Not for money."

Bill said sadly, "She's warned him."

"Pity," said Bob. "Only thing left is work. This way lad."

Bill gave Smiler a nod and a wink and went out of the barn, and Bob took Smiler in hand, explaining very solemnly what he would be expected to do. For Smiler it presented no problems because it was going to be much the same work that he had been doing in Scotland. There were animals to be fed, cages and pens to be mucked out, bedding to be carried, and corn sacks and hay bales to be humped, and then helping in all the hundred and one seasonal jobs that had to be done around the farm.

The barn they were in was used as a store and a garage for the tractor and other farm implements. The other barn, which was fitted out with cages and pens, held the boarders which were in residence at the moment. Outside in the large field which ran from the back of the farm down to the brook, there were at the moment two donkeys, a shetland pony, and the house cow. Between the two barns was a short run of stables for the horses that would be coming during the off season. At the moment they were empty. Bill explained that he and Bob, after they had left work and gone up to their cottage, had been taking it in turns to come down around ten o'clock at night to see that everything was all right in the barn which housed the birds and animals. Now, since Smiler was on hand in the farm, this was to be his duty. Before he went to bed he would make a last inspection and, if he heard a commotion at night, he would have to go out to attend to any trouble.

Smiler decided that he liked Bob and Bill, though he found it difficult to know when they were being serious or pulling his leg. Up in his room after work where he was getting cleaned up and changed for supper Smiler decided, too, that it had been a lucky moment that had brought Jimmy Jago along the road at the right time to pick him up. "You were lucky, Samuel M.," he told himself. "And let's hope the Duchess is right about what she saw in the crystal ball."

When Smiler went down to supper he was surprised to find that Jimmy Jago was not there, though he had seen him around during the day.

"Has Mr. Jago gone off again?" he asked the Duchess.

"Yes, he has, Samuel," said the Duchess. "Jimmy goes and comes like the wind. He's got restless feet and he doesn't like a roof over his head long. He's always on the go, buying a bit here and selling a bit there, and God knows what else, and never an answer to a straight question. You'll get used to it."

"But Scampi's not gone."

"No –" she grinned – "I expect Yin wouldn't let him. Now eat your supper and, while you're doing it, tell me all about this business of yours of wanting to be a vet."

So Smiler, between mouthfuls, told her all about his ambition to be a vet. and then to marry Laura Mackay, his girl friend, who was going to have a farm one day so they could combine the two things. When he had finished, the Duchess eyed him severely and said, "With the education you tell me you've had, you've set yourself an uphill struggle – but that's all to the good when you're young. Well, if it's education you're after we'll have to see what we can do about it once you're settled in. Meanwhile, when you go up to your room, take this with you."

She put something on the table between them. It was a small model in coloured clays of a boy with fair hair, whose shoulders were hunched forward slightly, supporting a small pebble which he was carrying like a rucksack.

"What's that for, ma'am?"

"It's for you – but it isn't you, Samuel. It's that Johnny Pickering of yours."

"But – I don't understand?"

"It's more magic, Samuel. Not black magic, but good magic. He did you harm, he caused you all your trouble. He's got a bad conscience because no one can escape their conscience. I've put a spell on him. Not a bad one, but a naggling one." The Duchess tapped the tip of her large nose. "A niggling, naggling one. Keep it in your room and one day you'll find that pebble's come unstuck and tumbled off. That will be the day when things will begin to go right for you. You'll see."

"You really mean that, ma'am?"

"Of course. And you must really believe it, Samuel. Really believe it. You know why?"

"No, ma'am."

"Because the strongest part of all magic is belief. When that pebble falls . . . well, you'll see."

*   *   *

That night before he went to bed Smiler walked across to the second barn to see that the birds and animals were all right. (Later on he never bothered

31

to go down through the house, but would step out of his bedroom window on to the roof of the kitchen extension and then jump down to the path. To get back he always kept a couple of boxes handy to step up on so that he could reach the roof.)

He unlocked the small door of the barn with the key which was hidden under the water-butt. Bob had already conducted him around the inmates of the barn and he knew most of their names and some of their histories. He switched on the overhead light and walked down the length of the barn.

Just now most of the large pens and cages were empty. In one was a chimpanzee called Freddie who was convalescing from a bad attack of bronchitis and had been left there by a circus which had been touring the West Country. Freddie, curled up in a bed of hay, looked up as Smiler came to his cage, wrinkled his mask at him in a friendly gesture, and then piled hay over his head as if to indicate that he wanted no more disturbance. In a cage a little farther down was a black poodle bitch recovering from a broken foreleg. This was Mabel. Seeing Smiler she came out of her sleeping-box and walked across to him on her hind legs and thrust her muzzle between the bars and held out her plaster-bound foreleg for him to shake. Smiler fondled her muzzle, shook hands with her and sent her back to bed. In other pens and cages, all for some reason or other temporary lodgers, were animals from the menageries and children's zoos which travelled with the circuses; a barbary ram, a small honey bear, a porcupine and, in the end pen, a South American tapir which was stretched out on its side snoring like an old man.

On the other side of the barn were the bird cages. All of these were empty except for three. One held a griffon vulture, huddled on its perch like a dejected old lady with a shabby boa of feathers around her neck. Another held a pair of Indian mynah birds. As Smiler stood in front of their cage one of them opened a sleepy but bright eye, surveyed him, and then, giving a drowsy whistle, said, "Lord, look at the time! Look at the time!" whistled once more, and closed its eye. But of all the creatures in the barn, the bird in the third occupied cage was the one which interested Smiler most of all. It was a peregrine falcon.

Her name was Fria and Bob had told him that she had been taken from an eyrie in Wales – before she could properly fly – by a falconer who intended to train her. But the circumstances of his own life had changed after a while and he had given her to the Duchess. He had felt that this was the best thing to do because to have loosed her to freedom would only have meant her death. She had had no training in how to hunt for her food and her wings were stiff and incapable of long flight from lack of the exercise she would have had in the wild state.

Fria sat on her perch, eyes wide open, and watched Smiler. She was now over two years old and had long moulted into her adult plumage so that her whitish breast was streaked crosswise with grey, whereas before, her breast had been buff-coloured and streaked vertically with brown. Her back was now a deep blue-black. There was little

33

gloss or shine to her feathers and she looked a sorry sight. But for all this there was still a fierce dignity in the way she stared from fixed eyes at Smiler as though to prove that for all her captivity her spirit was still far from broken.

Smiler felt a lump rise in his throat as he eyed her. He didn't like to see animals in captivity at all, though he knew that it was inevitable that some had to be, especially those to whom freedom would mean death. But Fria moved him more than all the others. Of all creatures he loved birds because they seemed to carry the real meaning of freedom in their lives. In Scotland he had watched the high soaring of golden eagles and the lazy circling of buzzards, seen the strong, steady flight of geese and the wild aerobatics of green plovers, and before that, when he had first run away from approved school, watched the wing-trembling hover of kestrels over Salisbury Plain and the marauding swoop of sparrow-hawks along hedges and around trees as they chased their prey.

Now, watching Fria, he wondered if she could remember back to the days of her eyrie life, to the moment when her wings were growing strong enough almost to the point of lifting her into flight alongside her falcon mother and her tiercel father . . . to take her up into the freedom of the air where she would be taught to stoop and prey and slowly gain a mastery of the air which would have been her real life. It was something he didn't like to think about.

He moved away, switched off the light and locked up the barn. As he went to his bed, because

34

all his recently passed troubles and adventures had, without his knowing it, begun to mature him, to change the boy of near sixteen to the beginning of manhood, he told himself that although Nature was full of death and cruelty it was a savagery that was without real evil. But the cruelty of man towards animals came not from any natural law but from the stupidity and thoughtlessness of men. Before he slept he told himself, "Samuel M., things should be different, they really should. And they could be if people knew how to care." For a while he even wondered whether he could really bear to stay here where so many animals were cooped up and then decided that he could because, at least, he could look after them even if he could never give them freedom.

When he awoke in the morning, however, he didn't feel half so gloomy about things and, if he had, the work he had to do through the day would have given him little time for brooding.

*   *   *

Within a month Smiler was feeling very much at home at Bullaybrook Farm. He knew the routine for all the jobs he had to do, and he did them well, for he was a good worker. The Duchess was pleased with him and so were Bill and Bob for, although they laughed and joked and pulled his leg, when it came to work they would not tolerate a half-done, sloppy job. In his spare time and at the week-ends Smiler, too, had begun to discover the country around the farm. In the store barn was an

35

old bicycle which had been bought in some deal by Jimmy Jago. Smiler put it in order and explored the surrounding lanes and the brook and river valley on it.

And in that month the shape and purpose of Smiler's life began to be defined. The Duchess had a talk with the local veterinary surgeon who came now and then to treat sick or ailing animals. After he had gone she explained to Smiler (though he knew some of this already) that he would have to study for the General Certificate of Education, first at the Ordinary level and then at the Advanced level – in which he would need two or three passes. When this was done he could apply for admission to one of the Universities which provided courses leading to degrees in veterinary science or veterinary medicine and surgery. Once he had a degree it would give him the right to be registered in the Register of Veterinary Surgeons and to membership of the Royal College of Veterinary Surgeons and the right to practise the profession in the United Kingdom. Apart from studying general subjects, Smiler would eventually have to tackle chemistry, physics and biology.

Listening to her, Smiler felt swamped by the prospect of the task ahead and his face showed it.

The Duchess chuckled and said, "Cheer up, Samuel. You can go a long way in small steps if you've plenty of time ahead of you – and you've got that. Fix your eye on the first mountain-top and forget the ones that lie beyond. Their turn will come."

Grinning ruefully, Smiler asked, "How am I

goin' to get up the first mountain, ma'am? I never did much at school."

"That's your fault. But it's never too late."

To prove it the Duchess arranged with a friend of hers, a retired schoolmaster in a nearby village, to start giving Smiler lessons two evenings a week in general subjects. Twice a week Smiler cycled to the village and was coached by the retired schoolmaster, a Mr. Samkin. Every day thereafter Smiler had to find time, either before or after supper, to work at a small table in his own room. Since the nights were now drawing in as October passed he didn't mind so much, but he wondered how he would stick it when the winter passed and spring and summer came, and all the springs and summers of the years ahead when the evenings were drawn out and full of invitation to go abroad into fields and woods. The only answer he could find was to tell himself, "If you want something bad, Samuel M., then you got to work for it. The great thing is not to think about it too much, but take it step by step like the Duchess says."

Smiler's birthday came and he was sixteen. Jimmy Jago was at home for it and gave him a good second-hand watch. "Now you're a working and studying man, my lad, you must value time. It's like water under a bridge. Once gone you can't bring it back." The Duchess gave him a thick sweater she had knitted herself, a stormproof jacket for the winter, and a fountain pen for writing up his notes because Mr. Samkin was old-fashioned enough to value good writing and turned up his nose at biros and self-propelling nonsenses like that. And Bill and Bob – not without design – gave him an old twelve-bore, single-barrelled shotgun, promised to provide the cartridges for it, and to teach him how to use it, so that from then on he could shoot the pigeons and rabbits around the farm for the table and also for feeding Fria – and relieve them of the job. When Smiler asked about having a licence for it, Bob looked at him (or it might have been Bill), winked, and said, "We'll meet that fence when we come to it. But remember – if we ever see you handle that gun anyway different from what we're goin' to show you, then you get your backside beaten and you'll be thrown in the Bullay brook."

But the best present of all was a letter from Laura Mackay which the Duchess gave him when they were alone. Before he had opened it, Smiler – blushing a bit – asked, "But how could she write to me . . . she don't know my address?'

The Duchess shook her head, setting her red curls dancing, and said severely, "Not 'don't know', boy. 'Doesn't know'. Mr. Samkin would give you stick for that. And how your girl knows your address is my business – there's not a county in the whole of this Kingdom where I don't have friends. Now up to your room and read it before you start work."

Smiler ran up to his room and sat by the window and read it.

Dear Sammy,
    An old gypsy man called by the other forenoon when Mum and Dad were out. He made

38

me swear some sort of secret daft rigmarole and then told me where you were. So I'm writing and no one will ever know unless you say so, and I wish I could come down to see you. And you can write to me because if Mum and Dad saw the letter they would never ask questions and anyway they would never give you away, not after everything. I hope you are keeping well as everyone here is, including the Laird and Bacon that is still with him. I miss you a lot, though I think you were a daft loon to go on the run again, but then you always thought you knew best. Look after yourself.

Yours,
Laura

P.S. Don't forget you promised to ask a certain question one day.   XX

Smiler read it through twice and each time little shivers of pleasure ran through him. Then he took his new fountain pen and a sheet of paper eager to answer the letter right away – but the excitement was too much for him. He just couldn't keep his bottom still on the chair and his right hand shook. He wrote "Dear Laura" – and then was stuck. He'd never written a letter to a girl in his life. Then he remembered one of the first things Mr. Samkin had told him: "Before you put anything to paper, first of all think about it, then think about it again, get your mind settled about what you're going to say – and then write. Many a man has ruined himself by a few ill-considered scrawls of ink on a piece of paper."

Smiler got up, went out of the window, across the kitchen roof and into the far barn. He walked the length of the cages and pens and finished in front of Fria. This now had become a ritual with him. It was always with Fria that he finished up. As he stood there one of the mynah birds opened an eye, whistled, and called, "Oh, look at us! Look at us!" But Smiler scarcely heard the bird.

Fria, her dark-brown eyes wide open, watched Smiler. She sat there, her breast feathers slack and shabby, the slate-blue feathers of her wings loosely laid, lacking the taut, steely compactness which would have marked a healthy bird like a coat of mail. There was a dinginess to the dull yellow of the cere at the base of her beak and of her long-taloned feet. The only feeling of power and wildness in her came from the stance of her head, in the unflinching gaze of her eyes bracketed by the black cheek-marks curving downwards. She knew Smiler now. It was he who fed her with pigeons, rabbit pieces, and the bodies of the barn mice caught in the traps which were around the place. She knew him, too, because he moved always without any sudden movement. Since he had come he had changed the bathing-tray in her cage for a wider, shallower one which she preferred. Now she bathed each day whereas before she had known no regular desire for the cleanliness which all peregrines love.

Standing before her, touched as he always was at the sight of her, Smiler said softly, "Fria . . . Fria . . ." The falcon made no movement. "Fria, I've had a letter from Laura . . . all the way from

Scotland. And one day I'm going to be a vet. and I'm going to marry her. I am. I promised to ask her. Not yet, of course. Not never – I mean, not ever – until I'm a real vet. And I'm going to be because everyone's helping me. That's good, isn't it? Maybe . . . well, perhaps I'll be able to think of something that . . . well, something that I can do for you, old girl."

Fria closed her eyes. She shut Smiler out. She shut everything out, closing out the world, drawing back into the limbo of her own unfathomable nature.

Smiler went quietly out and switched off the light.

*   *   *

Bob and Bill gave Smiler lessons in shooting and he soon became a fairly competent shot and – after one or two lapses, when he did get his backside kicked but was not thrown into the brook – a very safe handler of a gun. Although he didn't like killing things he now shot rabbits and wood pigeons and justified it because he knew that they were for the pot and for the griffon and Fria. But everything else was safe from him.

One day as he was pushing his bicycle up the hill from the farm a white minicar with a police sign on it pulled up alongside him. A youngish-looking policeman with a red, plump face leaned out.

"Hullo, there – you're Sammy, aren't you, the Duchess's nephew?"

For a moment Smiler didn't know what to say.

41

Then remembering Mr. Samkin's edict, he thought for a moment or two, and said, "Yes, I'm Sammy."

The policeman smiled. "And I'm P.C. Grimble – not Grumble, though I do. Nice to meet you, Sammy, and a word of advice." He winked. "So long as you keep that twelve-bore on your own patch I don't know it's there and I don't want to know. But you step on the highway with it and . . . well, that's it." He winked again, and then drove off. And so Smiler began to learn that although the law is the law – as he well knew – there was in every country community a law within the law, but it was one which had to be strictly observed. That he was the Duchess's nephew was news to him but, since he now knew something of the way the Duchess could arrange things, he decided that there was no point in mentioning it to her.

So, through the autumn and into the winter, Smiler worked hard and studied hard. The leaves turned brown and gold and fell, leaving only the green plantations of fir and pine to stand black against the early sunset sky. The rains fell and the Bullay brook and the Taw were swollen with chocolate-brown spates from the run-offs and streams bringing down the rich red Devon soil. And, as the spates began to fall, so the salmon and the sea-trout ran high up the river and cleared the weirs to seek their spawning-grounds. Smiler, hedging in the meadows by the brook, would sometimes creep up and watch the hen salmon cutting at their gravelly redds in the spate-cleared water while the cock fish hovered close by, ready to fertilize the eggs with their

cloudy milt. He grinned to himself when sometimes a cheeky little trout would dash in first – a
boy trying, as Bob or Bill said, to do a man's
work.

Now, by the time he had finished his work, it
was dark so that it was only at the weekends he
could get on his bicycle and explore the country
around or go for long walks – which was what he
preferred most to do. But, being young and not
wedded to the habit of regular sleep, there were
times when even after the day's labour there was
an itch in his limbs for movement. Sometimes,
after checking the creatures in the barn at night,
he would delay going back to bed and in moon-
light or clear starlight go off for a tramp for an
hour or two. It only took a little while for his eyes
to become accustomed to the dark and he moved
quietly and unobtrusively and was well rewarded.
He soon found where the nearest badgers had their
sett, knew the fox earths, and the trees where the
kestrels and buzzards roosted. He was no longer
startled when a barn owl ghosted silently by him
over the short field-stubble. His hair no longer
stood on end almost when a little owl shrieked
suddenly. The dogs on the neighbouring farms
knew him and now, when they scented him, never
bothered to bark, and there were dozens of places
where the pheasants roosted and it would have
been easy for him – had he been a poacher – to
raise a hand and take one. But Smiler preferred
just to be out, to be an inhabitant of a night-time
world which few other people knew. He knew the
track that came down the hill by the farm which

the travelling otters used when they came over country to reach the brook and so to the Taw, and the places in the clumps of cotton-grass where the jack-snipe bedded down. But the place he liked to go to most at night, particularly if there were a moon, was Highford House.

Highford House was about a mile and a half from Bullaybrook Farm. To get to it Smiler would follow the brook up the valley for a while then cut up the valley side through rough pastures and woods, across a small lane, and through a long stretch of Forestry Commission land which overlooked the Taw valley. The house, which had been built in the latter part of the nineteenth century, stood on the top of a hill that flanked the west side of the river. Once it had been a splendid mansion standing in its own park and woodlands. Now it was derelict and only a broken shell of its former self. The roof had been stripped of its lead and tiles, the windows of the magnificent rooms were without glass, and all the grand oak staircases had been removed. The park had become pasture and the once well-kept gardens had been reclaimed by thorn, elderberry, and small saplings of beech and oak. No formal flowers remained but the primroses, cowslips and other spring flowers had come back, and in autumn it was a riot of willow-herb and balsam. Built of great greystone blocks, it straddled the hilltop with its back to the woods, stranded like the skeleton of some long-dead monster. The winding drive that led out to the road was overgrown and hard to pick out. The once carefully kept rides of rhododendrons and azaleas had become a jungle and a sanctuary for all sorts of birds and animals. The jackdaws, kestrels and owls knew its broken roof parapet and crumbling walls and nested among them. Badgers and foxes over the years had burrowed to the wide maze of cellars that lay under the falling rubble, and grass snakes and adders in summer sunned themselves on the fallen stone slabs. Just behind the house was a tall, redbrick tower, relic of some older house that had once crowned the hilltop. Parts of the stone stairway that twisted up the inside of the tower still remained. But after the first floor there were great gaps in it and anyone who moved inside was in danger of setting off falls of brick and stone from higher up the tower. It rose high above the old house and the wilderness of woods and derelict park and from its top miles of the curving valley of the Taw could be seen, a valley where road, river and railway kept company, parted, and moved companionably together again as they ran northwestwards to Barnstaple and the sea.

It was here one December night that Smiler, still restless after a day's work and an evening's study, made his way to what he called his "thinking-place". This was the wide parapet ledge of the roof at the back of the house. He reached it by climbing the stout stems of an old ivy and, once ensconced, he could look down into the rubble-filled shell of the house or across the wilderness that had been a formal garden to the redbrick tower. Though his eyes and ears were always wide awake for the movement of a night bird or animal, the squeak of a field mouse or the scrape of a rat or rabbit, he would let himself go off into a reverie, imagining the times when all his troubles would be over, his father back and he well on the way to being a vet. Sometimes, a shadow amongst the other shadows of the old house, he would just sit and dream and later hardly know what his dreams had been. Now and then he would even go over in his mind all he was learning from Mr. Samkin – but not often.

He was sitting there this night, one of sharp frost, the fields already hoared and the stars blinking sharply through the cold air, warm in his sweater and storm jacket, when he heard a noise come from the inside of the house which he had never heard before. From below him, but away near one of the empty front windows of the ground floor, he heard the sound of something metallic suddenly ring out. Just for a moment or two he was startled and felt the quick prick of fear tingle his scalp. Although there was always a friendly feeling about the place, despite its ruined and lonely state, his mind leapt to the thought of ghosts and strange spirits. But a moment later he forgot them because clearly to his ears came a decidedly human grunt and a man's voice said crossly, "Next time bring a bugle and blow it."

Two men came into view, picking their way across the rubble below, clearly lit by the wash of starlight that flooded through the gaping roof. Moving quietly they crossed to the front window and paused there, surveying the stretch of wild pasture outside. The smaller of the two men carried a sack or a workman's tool-bag slung over his shoulder and Smiler guessed that something had probably fallen from this to make the noise he had heard.

The man with the tool-bag slipped through the window and was gone. The other man remained, as though waiting to watch that the other got unobtrusively away before he too left. One side of his face was clear in the starshine and Smiler saw that it was Jimmy Jago. For a moment his instinct was to call out to him, but he checked himself. He knew by now something of the ways of the Duchess and Jimmy and Bob and Bill. They were circus and Romany people and their ways were secret, even magic, and they lived by different rules than ordinary people.

At that moment Smiler was glad of Mr. Samkin who was making him read Kipling and remembered some lines from the last poem they had done –

If you wake at midnight, and hear a horse's feet,
Don't go drawing back the blind, or looking in
the street,
Them that asks no questions isn't told a lie,
Watch the wall, my darling, while the
Gentlemen go by!

So, Smiler sat where he was, a shadow in the angle of a ruined parapet ledge. And below, Jimmy Jago waited like another shadow. Then, from outside, there suddenly came the double note of a wintering curlew, or so Smiler thought it was until he saw Jimmy move, drop something among the rubble to the left of the window, and then slide out into the night. He knew that it had been an all-clear signal from the other man, who, he felt, might easily from his appearance have been either Bob or Bill.

To be on the safe side, Smiler sat where he was for fifteen minutes by his birthday watch – hands luminous – the present of Jimmy. He wondered, though he knew it was none of his business, what Jimmy was doing up here when only that morning he had supposedly driven off in his shabby old car on a dealing trip for two or three days. One thing was clear: neither of the men were poaching for there was nothing in the house to poach.

When he thought the coast was clear Smiler climbed down and went into the house. He picked his way across the broken rubble and stones of the floor to the window. Lying on the ground to one side of it was the object Jimmy had dropped.

Smiler picked it up. He stared at it puzzled. It was a very small broom or besom made of bunched hazel twigs bound together with a couple of twists of binder twine. Although it had no long wooden hazel pole for a handle it was a miniature of the hazel besoms that he used sometimes to sweep the floor of the barns.

Smiler studied it, shook his head in bafflement, and then told himself, "Samuel M., Jimmy's business is Jimmy's business and he's your friend."

He put the besom back where he had found it. But all the way home – although he knew it was none of his business – he just kept wondering what on earth anyone should want a besom for in a ruined old mansion that it would have taken an army of men and builders to bring back to its former glory.

48

3

ᕫ All Kinds of
Monkey Business ᕫ

It was three days before Jimmy Jago showed up at the farm again. He returned after supper and while Smiler was studying in his room he could hear him and the Duchess talking in the kitchen. It was not possible to hear what they said, but he had the impression that now and again some sort of argument was going on between them. However, Smiler, who knew what it was to be in trouble of his own, wisely decided that other people's affairs were nothing to do with him unless he were invited to share them. He sagely decided to say nothing and keep his own counsel – but this could not keep him from the use of his eyes.

Three times before Christmas arrived he sat on his parapet ledge at Highford House and saw the two men leave, always around the same time. Now, when he went up there – which was less often as winter gripped the valley – he always looked to see if the hazel besom lay by the window. If it did he was content to stay. But if the besom was not in its place, then he quietly made off.

He wrote to Laura regularly now and took a great deal of trouble over his letters so that they should be grammatically correct. It annoyed him sometimes that Laura did not write as often as he did, but when he taxed her with it she wrote back and told him ". . . not to be a daft loon. Do you think I've got nothing else to do all day but sit and write letters? And anyway you only write to me so much because you want to show off your grammatics."

Smiler also wrote to Albert a couple of times without giving his address. He got Jimmy Jago to post the letters well away from Devon while he was on his travels.

Through all this, Smiler went twice a week to Mr. Samkin who lived in the village at the head of the brook valley. But, although Smiler studied hard, he was not as happy at Mr. Samkin's as he had been. Mr. Samkin had taken on another student for extra coaching. This was a sixteen-year-old girl from the village called Sandra Parsons whose father was the local postman. Sandra had fair hair, blue eyes, a nice but slightly hooky nose, and a funny sort of giggle of a laugh which Smiler found irritating. But the chief thing that annoyed him was that Sandra was too friendly towards him. She so often found excuses to cycle down to Bullaybrook Farm and talk to him, when he should have been working, that he took to hiding when he saw her coming. On a Sunday, with two or three other girls, she would walk down and they would hang about the small stone bridge over the brook and, when he went off for a walk, follow him, giggling and laughing. But he had to admit that while they were at Mr. Samkin's Sandra was entirely serious and attentive to the instruction being given. Once in a fit of pique when Sandra spoilt one of his walks by joining up with him he called her nose "a hooky beak". Instead of being put out she laughed and said, "Oh, Sammy – that just shows how uneducated you are. It's an aristocratic nose. All the Parsons are descended from the King of the Barnstaple Treacle Mines. I suppose you'll tell me next that you didn't know treacle comes from a mine?"

Smiler groaned inwardly. There was nothing he could do but tolerate her, avoid her as much as possible, and feel more determined than ever to stick to his vow not to go to her Christmas party which she began to talk about well in advance.

By the time Christmas arrived there were a few horses in the stable, a couple of rosin backs and a small black pony which, given encouragement by Bill and Bob when it was in the yard, would go up on to its back legs and waltz and pirouette across the cobbles.

Christmas came with the first light fall of snow and a frost that made the ground bone-hard and lapped the fringes of the Bullay brook with a rim of ice. Jimmy Jago was at home for Christmas and Bill and Bob came down to have Christmas dinner with them all. Afterwards they all sat around the fireplace and exchanged presents. Smiler one week-end had gone on the train to Barnstaple to buy his presents for people – and had been considerably hampered in the expedition because Sandra had got wind of it and turned up on the train with two other girls. It had seemed to him that every time he turned a street corner or went into a shop there they would be. The best Christmas present Smiler had was a quiet word from Jimmy Jago before Bill and Bob arrived.

Jimmy said, "Never mind how, but I got a mate of mine to ask at the shipping company about your Dad. Seems he missed his boat at Montevideo because he went up in the hills for a two-day trip and got fever at the hotel where he was staying. He was in hospital up there for a couple of days before they realized he was from a ship."

"But he's all right now, isn't he?"

"Of course he is. But that isn't the half of it. Montevideo wasn't his lucky place. Just as he was getting over the fever, he slips on the tiles of the hospital corridor and breaks his leg." Jimmy grinned. "Would you say your old man is accident-prone?"

"It's news to me," said Smiler.

"Well, not to worry. Everything's all right. The company have taken care of him. He's on another of their ships now. It picked him up on its way to Australia. My mate couldn't find out when it's due back in this country. He didn't like to be any nosier in case the company began to wonder what he was so interested for."

"Oh, gosh, Mr. Jimmy – I'm glad he's all right. I mean, I knew he had to be, but it's nice to know. Thank you very much."

And the worst present of a kind was a Christmas card from Sandra Parsons. Inside it was a formal invitation to Smiler to attend her party on the night after Boxing Day. When he groaned about it the Duchess, with a warm glint in her eyes, said, "You're growing up, Sammy. You've got to learn that there are a lot of things you have to do in life out of politeness which you don't want to do. But I'll let you into a secret. Most of them usually turn out to be very pleasant. You write a nice *thank you* and say you'll go." She winked. "But there's no need to tell Laura about it if you don't want to."

The Duchess was right, of course. When Smiler went to the party it took less than half an hour for his initial reticence and shyness to wear off. Then he began to enjoy himself. Mr. and Mrs. Parsons were warm-hearted, friendly people and soon made him welcome. And Sandra and her friends, now that he was amongst them and part of their accepted company, seemed less giggly and stupid than he had thought. They played games and danced to a record player and Smiler – who had not done much dancing in his life, but had a natural sense of rhythm – soon picked up the steps required of him. Although it was not part of his choosing, Smiler found that he danced with Sandra more than with the other girls and, in some mysterious way, when games were played he found himself partnered by her or on her side. This, without his knowing it, made Smiler an enemy – a big, well-built farmer's son of eighteen called Trevor Green who regarded Sandra as his girl friend. He was far from pleased at the way Sandra and a few of the other girls had taken to the fair-haired, freckle-faced Smiler. Trevor Green was not the kind who brought his grievances out into the open. Also, he had enough intelligence to realize that if he showed his jealousy of Smiler openly then it would do him no good with Sandra and might – in the way of many females – merely provoke her to a more galling display of her liking for Smiler.

Trevor Green, from the day of the party, worked secretly against Smiler. Sometimes in the darkness of early evening he would walk through the brook fields and leave gates open so that the cattle strayed. Another night he crept into the barnyards and punctured both tyres on Smiler's bicycle with a fine bradawl so that Smiler would not suspect sabotage. He worked in the dark and in the way the country folk used to think the bad-tempered pixies worked when they wanted to make trouble and more work for those they disliked. He opened the hatch-gate of the disused leat which had once served the old Bullaybrook Mill. The brook was in spate and the water raced down the old leat, poured through a broken bank above the barns, and flooded the yards and the stables one night. Quietly and stealthily as the New Year came in and January wore away through wintry, roaring days of wind and rain, Trevor Green spaced his mischief and caused Smiler a great deal of extra work. But in the way of life, and without knowing it, he at last did something which, though it caused Smiler trouble and worry to begin with, in the end gave Smiler great pleasure and joy.

One night after Smiler had made his last inspection of the animals in the barn and had returned to his bedroom, Trevor Green crept up to the barn, took the key from under the water-butt, and let himself in. He closed the door and switched on the light. The only windows in the barn were at the far end and could not be seen from the house.

He went down the row of cages and pens and opened the doors of the Barbary ram's pen and that of Freddie the chimpanzee. On the other side of the barn he opened the cages of the griffon, the mynah birds and of Fria. None of the animals paid much attention to him. An eye was opened from sleep and then closed. Fria stared graven-faced at him, eyes unblinking. Within a few minutes he was gone, chuckling to himself, picturing the trouble Smiler would have in the morning when he arrived and found birds and animals loose in the barn.

It was a stupid trick, the product of a small, jealous mind – and it would have been a complete failure had it not been for Freddie. Most of the animals were so used to their captivity that they were content to stay where they were and go on sleeping. So was Freddie for a long time. He was warm and comfortable in his straw bed. He had cocked an uncurious eye at Trevor as he passed, yawned, and drifted away into sleep again.

But at four o'clock in the morning Freddie woke and sat up blinking. That the barn lights should be on was unusual, and the unusual now stirred Freddie's curiosity. He saw that the door of his cage was open and shambled over to it, long arms swinging, his knuckles brushing the ground, his large, old man's mouth working soundlessly as though in silent irritation at the break in barn routine. One of the mynah birds cocked an eye at him and, giving a sleepy whistle, said, "Lord, look at the time! Look at the time!" Freddie gave a pout of his thick lips at the bird, scratched his head and then dropped to the floor. Grunting to himself, he made a little tour up his side of the barn, absent-mindedly picked up a piece of wood from the floor and rattled it along the bars of the tapir's cage. At the far end of the building was a flight of wooden steps that led to a loft. Freddie went up the steps and sat on the top rung. The trap-door leading into the loft was closed. He banged on it as though it were a drum for a while and then dropped from the top steps to the ground in an easy movement. He enjoyed the exercise so much that he went up the steps and repeated the performance. He walked down the length of the bird-cages to the open door of the griffon's cage.

The griffon, head sunk between its shoulders, eyes half open, followed his movements, its great beak swinging slowly. Freddie raised his head to it, wrinkled his face, and chattered gently through clenched teeth. He banged his piece of wood to and fro across the open doorway. The griffon shook out its shabby plumage and sidled along its perch a few inches.

Freddie climbed up the bars of the cage and sat on top of it. Experimentally he reached down through the bars with his piece of wood and tried to touch the griffon.

Reluctantly the griffon flopped down from its perch to the cage floor like a disgruntled old woman and shuffled into a far corner. Freddie carried on a little chattering conversation to himself and then crossed over to the top of the mynah birds' cage. They turned their long beaks up to him defensively and half opened their wings to a threatening posture. One of the birds took off from its perch, swooped through the open door and flew up to the window ledge at the far end of the barn where it settled, whistled, and called, "Say it again! Say it again. . . . Oh, clever bird!"

Freddie, stirred now by his unusual liberty, chattered with excitement and sidled quickly along the top of the cages, moving in a sideways, hump-backed posture. He did a little jumping dance on top of the griffon's cage. Then he dropped to the floor, ran along the barn, climbed the loft steps on the rear side, swung from a rung with one foot and dropped to the floor. He landed outside Fria's cage.

Fria, wide awake now and disturbed by all the unusual movement, looked down at him and gaped silently through her strong hooked beak. Freddie rattled his stick against the open door. Fria, alarmed, edged along her perch to the side of the cage. Freddie, grunting, hauled himself up into the open doorway of the cage and walked in, keeping well away from Fria. He leaned over her shallow tin bath and took a drink of the water. Then, with a sudden movement, he seized the side of the bath and up-ended it. Water streamed all over the floor and the bath went half-rolling, half-sliding towards Fria. Freddie gave a sudden scream of excitement and leapt after it.

Fria moved with her characteristic swift peregrine shuffle across her perch. As Freddie came after her, waving his stick, she launched herself towards the open door. She flew awkwardly and weakly, losing height and landed clumsily in a heap in the dust and straw alongside the ram's pen.

Freddie sat in the doorway of her cage and watched her. Fria straightened herself up, shook her wings into place, and stared at him.

Highly excited now, Freddie did a chattering dance in the doorway, dropped to the ground, and went after Fria. Alarmed, Fria ran along the ground, wings half open for flight. As Freddie came swiftly for her, she launched herself again. This time her wings beat more strongly as she strove to lift herself above the pursuing chimpanzee.

She made the top rung of the barn ladder, hitting it clumsily, and just managing to hold on with her talons. Freddie eyed her from the bottom of the ladder, grunting with pleasure at this newfound game. Then he went up after her.

Fria spread her dark slate-grey wings and flew awkwardly half the length of the barn, aiming for the top of the griffon's cage. She missed it, tried out of some dim instinct for the mechanics of flight to check herself with a braking of her wings, hit the side of the cage and fell to the floor. The mynah birds, now thoroughly astir, shrieked and whistled and Freddie came chattering after her.

Frightened, her heart beating with near-panic strength, Fria jumped into the air as Freddie neared her. Fear gave her enough strength to take

58

her up and into a clumsy half-turn. She came out fo it awkwardly and flew in slow wing-beats down the barn to the loft steps again. After her, delighted with the game, came Freddie.

It was Freddie's delight in his antics that benefited Fria. In her own cage she had never done more than exercise her wings now and then by flapping them as she sat on her perch, and using them to half-jump, half-fly to and from the cage floor. She had never known the pure wonder of a peregrine's real flight, knew nothing of the mastery of the air which is the supreme gift of the falcons, had never as an eyas stood ready for the first essay in flight on some eyrie lip with a deep drop below and the freedom of the skies above, nerving herself for the first launching into space to take her place alongside tiercel and falcon winging and wailing encouragement as they quartered the air a few feet out from the eyrie. Her wing muscles were stiff, unused, and un-trained in co-ordination. When it came to flying she had almost everything to learn. With Freddie pursuing her now, she was forced into a series of panic lessons. For the next half-hour Freddie kept up his assaults and each time Fria was forced to make her escape, and each time she did some little of the stiffness and awkwardness of her wings dropped from her.

In the end whether from design, from the forced exercise of her natural wit, or from pure luck she escaped him by finding the ledge of an old bricked-up window high above the door which led into the barn, where Freddie, grumbling and

59

chattering with frustration, could not reach her.

She sat there trembling with nervous and physical exhaustion while Freddie danced below her for a while. Then, as though tired of the taste of freedom, Freddie shambled off down the barn, jumped into his cage and bundled himself up in his straw bed and slept.

The mynahs which had escaped swooped down and into their cage. Fria sat on her ledge and slowly the fear she had known began to leave her. But as it died away, so did some part of the old Fria. For the first time in months she had known a kind of freedom and its unusual touch had stirred something in her spirit.

*   *   *

Smiler was the first into the barn the next morning. One glance told him that things were not right. The light was still on and, more obviously, Freddie was sitting on the lowest rung of the loft ladder placidly chewing at an onion – his favourite food – which he had taken from a string of these vegetables which was hung up over the grain-store bin beneath the far window.

Freddie looked up, gave Smiler a welcoming grunt, and then shambled across to him, holding the half-eaten onion in his mouth. Before Smiler could do anything Freddie shinned up him, clamped one long arm around his shoulders and nuzzled his face into Smiler's neck affectionately, almost choking him with the strong odour of onion.

Smiler took one look down the row of cages and saw the mischief that had been done. With Freddie in his arms he went down the barnside, shutting pen doors and cages. He prised Freddie from him and put him in his cage, where he retired happily to his straw bed to finish the onion.

Smiler crossed the barn and closed up the griffon's and the mynah birds' cages and then stood in front of Fria's cage. It was empty and the upturned bath lay across the damp boards at the back of the cage. Smiler, feeling angry at whoever had come into the barn to cause trouble, turned slowly round with a grim face. In the dim, early morning light from the far window he saw Fria sitting on her ledge about sixteen feet from the ground. Her eyes were open, watching him, but her head was sunk into her shoulders and her feathers had been shaken out so that she looked like some disreputable old owl.

Smiler stood there, not knowing what to do. He had left the barn door open and he knew that he would have to go back along the length of the barn to close it before he could attempt to catch Fria. Once the barn door was shut he could un-hook the loft ladder and set it against the wall, take a sack and go up to Fria. With luck, he could throw it over her before she moved. Watching her out of the corner of his eye, he began to move slowly up the barn. Fria watched him unmoving.

With a feeling of relief Smiler reached the door and shut it. Trying to keep his movements easy and unalarming, he found a sack and then un-hooked the loft ladder. Very slowly he raised it against the wall. As the top of the ladder came to rest a foot below her Fria suddenly half-flapped her wings and, lowering her head, bated at the ladder top below her. Smiler kept still and waited until she had calmed down. Then very slowly he began to climb the ladder. As far as Fria was concerned he would have gladly let her go to her freedom had she been able to fly properly and look after herself by killing, but he knew that once she was loose outside she would have only the slimmest chance of survival.

Smiler crept up the ladder, making a soft clicking sound at the back of his throat – something which for weeks now he had taken to doing when he fed Fria. It was a sound she understood. It meant food. Smiler prayed that she was hungry enough now to stay where she was in the hope of being fed.

When he was four rungs from the top of the ladder Smiler halted. Taking his weight on his feet, his knees pressed against a ladder-rung to give him a firm balance, he slowly got both hands to the sack and with an unhurried movement spread it wide so that he could swamp the falcon with it.

Slowly he began to raise the sack and Fria watched as it came level with her feet. Then, just as Smiler was poised to make his bid to capture her, from far down the barn Freddie, his onion finished, and greedy for another, suddenly began to chatter loudly and shake at the bars of his cage. The sound disturbed Fria. All her fears during the night chase had been associated with it. As Smiler made a lunge to cover her, she ran sideways along the ledge and launched herself downwards. Smiler, just saving himself from falling from the ladder, turned and saw her wing clumsily down the barn towards the far window. She rose awkwardly to the light coming through. Then, realizing it offered no escape, she made a scrabbling turn, so close to the glass that her left wing flight feathers swept away an accumulation of old spiders' webs. She lost a couple of feet on the turn and, the panic she had known during the night returning to her, she swept back up the barn. She was faced with an awkward turning maneuver to avoid the end wall of the barn. She made a mess of the turn, hit the wall lightly, and tried to cling to it. For a moment or two she hung, wings beating, her talons scrabbling against the surface for a hold, spread-eagled like some awkward bat. Then she fell away sideways, and flew straight for the barn door, half-dazed with fear and shock.

At that moment the door opened inwards. Bob Old stood on the threshold. Fria dived towards him, swerved slowly to one side, and flew out into the open as Smiler gave a far-too-late, warning shout.

Outside a strong west wind, damp with the promise of rain to come, swept across the brook valley. For the first time Fria felt the living, pulsing power of moving air cushioned under her wings and was tossed up out of control like a vagrant sheet of newspaper. She met the force with panic and wild wing-beats, and her beating wings took her up almost vertically across the face of the barn wall.

63

Just under the roof of the barn, and protected by a little gable roof of its own, was the loft doorway. Projecting from the top of the doorway was a stout wooden rafter with a pulley wheel attached to its end. Unused now, this projecting pulley beam had formerly served for hauling sacks of corn from carts below for storage in the loft.

As she beat frantically upwards Fria saw the overhang of the small gable roof and the long length of the pulley beam. From instinct rather than design she flew into the shelter of the little roof, raised her wings and settled with a desperate, scrambling movement of legs and talons on the beam. Once there she squared around slowly to face the force of the blustery wind.

Down below Smiler and Bob stared up at her.

Bob said, "How did she get free?"

Angrily Smiler said, "Some stupid devil got in the barn last night and opened some of the cages."

Bob considered this, and then said, "That don't surprise me. There's one or two around here don't altogether take to us. Circus folk, gypsies, didikys they know we are – and because they don't understand our ways they take a delight in being awkward."

"But what are we going to do about Fria, Mr. Bob?"

"Go up and open that loft door and just leave her. Come food time, put some out for her in the loft. When she's hungry enough she'll go in and then we can put the ladder up from here and close the doors on her. No trouble then."

"But say she flies off or gets blown off? She

64

doesn't know how to look after herself. She'll just die."

"Ay, she might, Sammy. But then again, she might not. Animals may not think like humans, but they've got their own kind of common-sense. She'll settle for herself what she wants to do – and my guess is that she'll come into the loft for food when she's hungry."

*   *   *

But Fria did not come into the loft, though Smiler did everything he could to get her back. That first day he opened the loft doors and put food and water on the broad sill of the hatch opening. When Fria saw him at the opening she shuffled along the pulley beam well out of reach, took a firm grip on the weather-worn wood and sleeked down her feathers to ease the wind resistance against her. Time and again, as Smiler worked, he came back to see her, but she scarcely moved her position on the beam all day.

That night the food and drink were left on the ledge and the loft doors open. A new and more secure hiding-place was found for the barn key. When Smiler made his night visit the food was untouched and the dark shape of Fria on her beam was silhouetted against the night sky.

For two days Fria did not move from her beam except to shuffle back under the protection of the small pent roof when it rained hard. She sat and watched the strangeness of the new world before her, like a medieval carving. There was nothing

65

wrong with her physically except that her body, her flight muscles and her talents were unused and untrained. Her eyes, which could take in the whole horizon without moving, except the little segment of the loft in her rear, were the wonder eyes of a falcon, nature's great gift to her kind. Her wide-ranging eyes had eight times the power of man's and a depth of focus that could show her the quick beat of a rook's wing miles away, the fall of a late leaf half-a-mile up the far valley side, and the movement of a foraging, long-tailed field-mouse through the winter grasses down by the brook.

Fria sat on her beam and watched this new world. She watched the movement of the cattle in the pasture, the quick flight of pigeons coming high over the valley woods, the movement of people and traffic now and then at the brook bridge, the rolling, changing shapes of the rain-clouds sweeping in from the distant sea, and the coming and going of Smiler and Bob and Bill and the Duchess about the farm. But there were two things she watched in those first days with special interest. At noon one day, when a scattering of sparrows were squabbling on the yard cobbles over a few handfuls of grain that had been spilled, a sparrow hawk came round the corner of the barn in a swift, low-flying, piratical swoop. As the sparrows rose in alarm, the hawk burst into their midst, did a half wing-roll and took one of the sparrows in its talons and flew on with it. Something about the hawk and the maneuver wakened some ancestral memory in Fria. Three times a day for the first two days Fria saw this maneuver and each time a sparrow was taken. And another bird wakened a response in her. Now and again a kestrel came quartering up the valley and hung over the pasture by the brook. Fria eyed it the first time, watched the wing-tip tremor of its poised hover and saw, as plainly as the kestrel could see, the movement of a winter foraging vole in the brookside grasses. When the kestrel plummeted with upraised wings and made its kill, Fria shuffled restlessly on her beam. She lowered her head, trod impatiently with her feet and uttered a faint call, a thin wail – *wickoo*, *wickoo* – that was barely audible. Again and again Fria watched sparrow hawk and kestrel in their hunting and always an excitement stirred in her which sent a swift tremble through her wings or made her lower her head and wail gently.

And during those days Smiler watched and worried about Fria. But on the morning of the fourth day he felt happier. Sometime, either during the night or at first light, Fria had moved down from her beam to the loft edge. One of the mice Smiler had taken in a barn trap was gone. Late that afternoon when he checked he saw that she had been down again and had taken a piece of meat from the food laid out for her. He saw, too, that the small bowl of drinking water he had set out was tipped over and he guessed that Fria had tried to take a bath in it.

From then on Fria began to eat regularly and Smiler would find her castings lying on the ground below the beam. When she was used to feeding,

Smiler began to move the food farther and farther back from the loft opening because he wanted to train Fria to go well back into the loft to eat, so that one day he and Bob would have a chance to set up the ladder and shut the doors on her before she could get back to her beam. But Fria was not to be tempted. When the food was set farther back into the loft she refused to eat for two days and Smiler put it back on the ledge of the loft opening.

He did this with a definite plan in mind. He explained it to the Duchess. "You see, I don't really want to catch her just to shut her up in her cage again. What good's that going to do her?"

"Well, she can't sit up on that pole for ever, Sammy."

"But that's it, ma'am. She won't. If I feed her regular——"

"Regularly."

". . . regularly, and she begins to get strong and . . . well, sort of more contented . . . Well, then maybe she'll fly. You know, take off on a little flight. But she'll always come back for her food, because she can't hunt for herself. Not, anyway, until she's a real good flyer. When she's like that – well, isn't there a chance she might start to hunt?"

"Well, I suppose there is. But not a strong one, surely?"

"Maybe not, but there is a chance and it's worth trying, ma'am. Gosh, I know if it was me and I could have the chance I'd take it. What kind of life is it just sitting in a cage?"

The Duchess eyed him silently for a moment,

pursing her plump lips, and then she said quietly, "Well, I'll tell you what, Sammy. Even though I'm an old circus hand and I'm used to animals in cages and being trained, I've got to admit that the older I get the less I like it. So from now on the responsibility is yours. You can have Fria. She's your property and you can decide what is best for her."

"Really, you mean that?"

"I do."

Smiler jumped up. "Oh, thank you, ma'am. Thank you." He moved to her, put his arms around her without thinking, and gave her a hug.

The Duchess chuckled. "Well, thank you, Sammy. It's a long time since any man did that to me. But remember, whatever you decide may be best for Fria, she may have ideas of her own. She's a woman. And women have minds of their own."

That night when Smiler made his late-night barn visit, he looked up at the dim shadow of Fria sitting on her beam and, since there was no one around to hear him, he said aloud, "All right, you old bird up there, you start doing something for yourself – and I'll help you all I can."

It was from that day that Smiler started to keep a diary. It was a secret diary which he began for a variety of reasons. He wanted to keep a record of all that might happen to Fria. He felt, too, that it would be a good exercise in improving his English.

His first entry read:

February 2nd. (I think). Started this diary at

Bullaybrook Farm, N. Devon. Fria belongs to me. Though of course she really belongs to herself but I am going to help and also get some books from the travelling County Library about peregrine falcons which in a way will be like helping in my vet. studies. Windy night, some rain. The Duchess is OK. So is Dad. So is Laura. And in a way so is Sandra. Bob says he can guess who did the barn job, but he won't tell me.

4

ᴑ *Two Under Instruction* ᴑ

During the next few days Fria was content to stay on her beam except for the times when she flew down to the loft ledge to eat or drink. Jimmy Jago came back to the farm for a couple of days and when Smiler showed him the falcon, he said, "Well, as long as she stays there she's safe from any farmer's gun. If I were you, too, Sammy, I wouldn't say anything about her to anyone. Somebody around here doesn't like us, lad. They might take a crack at her."

"What I'm hoping," said Smiler, "is that she'll pluck up courage and learn to fly properly and look after herself."

Jimmy cocked an eye at him. "And then what? Find a mate and raise a brood? That's what she should do but there's no chance of that. The falcons are dying out. There might be the odd pair out on the cliffs around Baggy Point but the breed is going and human beings are responsible. She might be happier free – but she'd be much safer in a cage."

"If you had the chance, Mr. Jago, and could catch her – would you put her back in a cage?"

Jimmy chuckled. "Good question. And the answer is – no. How often have you seen me go into the barn?"

"Not often."

71

"That's because I don't like to see anything caged up. The Duchess and I never quarrel about anything but that – things shut up in cages. No, I'm with you – give her a chance and, if she takes it, good luck to her."

From the County Library van, Smiler got some books on birds and read all about the peregrine falcons and, his interest roused, he got other books and began to understand something of the way the wild creatures of his country had to fight for their existence against the sometimes deliberate and sometimes careless ways that men put their lives in jeopardy. And, because he was determined to be a vet. one day, through his reading he made himself understand the careless ways in which death came to many birds because of the poisonous chemicals used in pesticides which were eaten on dressed seeds or contaminated insects by the small birds, and passed on to the predators like the hawks, owls and peregrine falcons when they ate their prey. The poisons from chemicals like Dieldrin, Aldrin, Heptachlor and DDT built up through the whole food chain of insects, rodents, small birds, wood pigeons and the fish in the seas and finally killed the preying birds at the end of the chain. Although he sometimes talked about this with Mr. Samkin, and asked his advice about books, he never mentioned Fria to him or to Sandra. Not that he distrusted them but he knew now how a careless remark could spread and he wanted Fria left alone to take her chance of freedom if she chose to do so. So far she showed no sign of doing this.

Every morning when he went out to the barn Fria would be sitting on her beam, either far out to enjoy the winter sun or drawn back under the small pent roof if the weather was bad. She ate and drank regularly now, and often, clinging to her beam, would raise and beat her wings as though she longed to let go and launch herself but could not find the courage. But some differences Smiler did notice in Fria. She ate more and her plumage was coming back into a better condition. She was so used to him, too, that when he came to the loft entrance she would move only the minimum distance along her beam to be out of his reach. Sometimes Smiler would stand and watch her for quite a long time, and he would talk to her in a soothing voice, but as the days went by there were times when he got angry with her and scolded her for not taking off and trying her wings. As an experiment he withheld her drinking and bath water for two days, hoping she would fly down to the brook, but Fria stayed where she was. Smiler, unable to be cruel, restored her water.

Yet, in the end, it was water which made Fria leave her beam. For many days she had watched the world around the farm and was familiar with it and with the passage of human beings and the creatures of the ground and the air. So far few other animals had marked her presence on the beam. The starlings and sparrows and the odd jackdaw had seen her and recognized the menace which was written in her shape and stance. They kept away from the front of the barn now. If the cohorts of rooks that had taken to wild aerobatics over the valley wood as the time for repairing old nests crept on had seen her they might have been bold enough to come down in ragged company and mob her into moving. So far she had escaped their sight. Fria saw and knew them all.

Most of all, though, she watched, particularly if the morning were sunny and there was a touch of added warmth in the air, the movement of the water in the brook. At the end of the first farm field the brook bank had been carried away by flood and the stream spread back in a wide half-moon over a gravelly shallow only a couple of inches deep. A restlessness which had been slowly growing in her was always more marked when she watched the sunlight rippling over the shallows, for although the air is the peregrines' first love and true element they all have a love, too, of water, of bathing and cleanliness. Smiler had provided her with a bath but Fria, although she used it now and then, did not like it. Her feet slipped on the smooth metal of the tray and she found it difficult to bob and dip her head under and send the water rolling over her mantle in the way which instinct demanded of her.

One windless, sunny morning in mid-February, Fria sat surveying the brook and the shallows. Suddenly, when no one was watching, she launched herself from the beam, gave a few slow beats of her scimitar-pointed wings and glided the two hundred yards down to the brook. She settled a little clumsily between two patches of cotton grass at the edge of the pool, raised her head to the sky, and then walked into the shallow water. With the gravel firm under her feet and nothing to block off her wide area of vision, she took a bath. The first she had ever known in freedom.

She dipped and bobbed her head under, letting the water roll back over her neck and down her wings. She loosened her breast feathers and plucked and preened at them under water. For five minutes she made her toilet and through every second, although she seemed relaxed, she was aware of all the movement around her. Then she walked out of the shallows, shook herself, gave a half-hearted preen of her breast, slid her beak down a couple of the primaries of her right wing and jumped free of the ground and began to fly back to the barn. There was neither wind nor obstacle for her to negotiate. Her wing muscles had grown a little stronger and less stiff with the limited liberty from her cage so that she flew up at a long angle easily and unhurriedly. A wood pigeon coming high and fast down the valley saw her and dropped like a plummet into a clump of ash trees by the brook bridge. The hens in the run at the back of the farm kitchen saw her and they froze into a crouch and waited for her to pass. Fria saw them all and more. She saw Bob on a tractor far down the valley, the flick of a jay's wing in the hedge that bordered the hill-road beyond the farm, and the lithe movement of a black mink quartering along the rabbit-holed hedge below the rooks' wood. But they meant nothing to her in terms of food or preying. She swung up to her beam, misjudged it a little, high shooting it, then corrected her flight and dropped awkwardly on to her accustomed perch. She sat there for the next fifteen minutes preening and combing her plumage. Fria had made her first voluntary move away from captivity.

*　　*　　*

That night another – and very different – move was being made for someone to escape captivity. The River Taw that flowed into the sea at Barnstaple began life in a lonely area of boggy marshland, seamed with a hundred small rivulets and streams, forty miles southwards on the high slopes of Dartmoor. A man who knew the river could – except for now and again making a quick road or rail crossing – pick his way easily from the source down to the first mud banks of its tidal reaches without, particularly at night, much fear of being observed or questioned. Jimmy Jago was such a man, and there were many others, river keepers, fishermen, country people and poachers.

This night Jimmy was high up in the moor, almost to the top of Taw Head, a wild expanse of mires and marshes where small streams and water gullies had cut deep into the heather-peat soil, a place where a man had to move carefully if he wanted to avoid going up to his waist in the boggy, treacherous ground. Though it was dark, with only starlight to guide him, Jimmy knew his way around from the reconnaissance he had made in the last months. To his left the great bulk of Hangingstone Hill lifted a long shoulder against the sky and then sloped gently southwards to the scarp of Whitehorse Hill. This was the very heart of the moor. Within a radius of two or three miles of this place rose many rivers, some to flow south to the English Channel and some north to the Atlantic . . . the Taw, the Okement, the Tavy, the Dart, the Teign and others.

Jimmy, with a heavy pack on his back, moved up the side of Hangingstone Hill until he came to a small outcrop of rock, its crest covered with whortleberry bushes. Underneath the overhang of the rock the ground had been scooped back and trod bare by generations of sheep that had used it for a refuge. There were three sheep in it now. They scattered as Jimmy appeared.

He went under the overhang and slipped off the pack. From inside it he took a sheet of thick polythene and wrapped the pack in it, binding the four corners into a tight twist at the top and cording them securely so that all dampness would be kept out. From his jacket pocket he took a small trowel. Squatting on the ground, he began to dig away at the hoof-packed earth. After an hour he had made a hole large enough to take the pack and deep enough so that when he scraped back the loose soil there was a good three-inch layer above it. The rest of the earth he scattered over the ground, stamping it down with his feet. In a couple of days the sheltering sheep would have packed it down even harder and no one – if by any unlucky chance anyone should come that way at this time of the year – would know the ground had been disturbed. Then he took the trowel and rammed it hard into the earth wall a few inches below the underside of the overhanging boulder. He forced it in until only the small circle of the top of the brown, work-worn handle showed like the knob of a root.

This done Jimmy backed out of the recess and looked around him. The night was far from silent. There was the incessant sound of water noises from the mires and small streams, the cough now and then of one of the sheep he had disturbed, the high call of a curlew and far away, from one of the lower valleys, the barking of a dog. But although Jimmy heard them it was without interest. There was only one concern in his mind at that moment, the demand of blood and kinship which in thought carried him eight miles farther south across the wild, unfriendly spread of the moor to the grim, grey jail at Princetown. He had done all he could. The clothes and provisions in the pack were there to be taken if the man for whom they were destined could ever reach them. Many men in their time had escaped from the prison working parties that laboured in the fields and quarries surrounding the jail, slipping off when the longed-for cover of heavy moorland mist suddenly descended. But to escape was one thing. A man then had to beat the moor, to find his way off it, avoiding all the roads because they were at once blocked with police patrols and barriers. The eight miles between Princetown and the spot where Jimmy now stood could for some men, particularly if they were city bred and the weather turned against them, just as well have been eight hundred.

Jimmy suddenly gave a little shiver of cold and

apprehension and then turned away northwards and began to work his way back to the lower slopes where the Taw after a few miles would find its stripling strength and form and begin the long flow to the sea.

*   *   *

Mr. Samkin, although he was nearing his seventies, was an active man, both physically and mentally. He was very short and broad-shouldered and the way he walked reminded Smiler very much of a bulldog. When he asked a question, too, he had a habit of shooting his head forward which increased the resemblance. His motto was work hard and play hard – but he insisted that work should be done before play. Smiler liked him, since Mr. Samkin never treated him as a school-boy, but as a young student with a brain and ideas of his own. Smiler soon took to speaking frankly about things and having decided opinions of his own, and Mr. Samkin encouraged this.

Once, for instance, Smiler grumbled about the dullness of some of the books which he had been set to read in his study of English literature. This applied particularly to Sir Walter Scott. In talking one evening after their tuition period was over and Sandra had gone, Smiler said, "I can't see, sir, why you should have to read something which doesn't interest you – like Sir Walter Scott. What good does it do you?"

"The good a thing does you, Samuel, isn't always apparent immediately. Anyway, why don't you like Sir Walter Scott?"

"I don't know, sir, but I don't."

With a humorous glint in his eye Mr. Samkin said, "That's not a good enough answer. All right, Samuel, this weekend you write me a five-hundred-word essay on your objections to reading Sir Walter Scott."

"Oh, sir . . ."

Mr. Samkin chuckled. "It won't kill you. And let me ask you this – have you ever read his *Marmion*?"

"That's a poem, isn't it, sir?"

"Yes."

"No, I haven't, sir. His books are bad enough."

"Well, perhaps you've missed something. Listen to this."

Mr. Samkin, with a sly twinkle in his eyes, recited:

We hold our greyhound in our hand,
    Our falcon on our glove;
But where should we find leash or band
    For dame that loves to rove?
Let the wild falcon soar her swing,
    She'll stoop when she has tired her wing.

Smiler, eyes wide, said impulsively, "Oh, I like that."

Mr. Samkin chuckled. "Of course you do. Because he's caught your special interest. So, I suggest you give Sir Walter Scott another chance – but you also do the essay. Good night, Samuel."

At the door Smiler turned and said, "You deliberately chose that bit, sir. About the falcon. Why?"

Mr. Samkin, beginning to pack tobacco into his pipe, said casually, "Oh, I keep my eyes open, Samuel. And – when my eyes aren't good enough – I use those."

He nodded to a side table where lay a pair of Zeiss binoculars of which Smiler had been aware almost from the first day he had started his tuition. He would have given anything for a pair like it.

Mr. Samkin went on, "Do me a good essay – and any day you want to borrow those you can have them."

"Oh, thanks ever so much, sir."

"I prefer 'Thank you very much'. And don't worry. I'm not a gossip."

Smiler went down the hill to the farm with Scott's words singing in his mind. *But where should we find leash or band for dame that loves to rove? Let the wild falcon soar her swing. . . .* If only she would, thought Smiler. If only she would and, while she was about it, learn to hunt and look after herself. He had already seen Fria fly down to bathe now and then. But that wasn't enough. Still . . . it was something.

*   *   *

But Fria, as February wore towards March and in the lee of sheltered banks a stub-stemmed primrose or two began to blossom, showed no inclination to soar. Nevertheless she was changing.

Most days now she flew confidently down to the shallows and bathed. Now and then, instead of pitching by the water, she would change her mind and beat round with a quicker rhythm in her wings, circle, and go back to her beam perch. Her wing muscles were stronger and a slow confidence in her flight powers was building in her. Once, too, as she stood in the cotton grass by the water, the movement of a beetle over the ground a foot from her caught her eye. With a reflex that had nothing almost to do with her, she jumped and snapped up the beetle in her beak. But once there, she held it for a moment or two and then let it fall. She was well fed, the beetle meant nothing to her in terms of hunger, so she dropped it.

Now, too, when she took her short flights she was noticed, but not by many humans. Mr. Samkin had seen her, it was true. So had the river bailiff as he came up the Bullay brook one day checking the spawning redds and keeping an eye open for dead salmon kelts. But the bailiff was like Smiler – he loved all animals and he kept his own counsel.

The birds and animals knew her now and they kept clear of her, crouching, hiding or going to cover if they were anywhere near her. Not even the rooks were tempted to interfere and mob her. They were busy with their nest-building and full of an exclusive excitement of their own as they robbed sticks from one another and began their mating flights and battles.

Only once did the rooks come near to approaching Fria. One mid-morning she launched herself from her beam and began to glide down to the water meadow. But the wind that morning was uncertain. Boisterous gusts would suddenly sweep down from the head of the valley towards the wood and, meeting it, would swirl in turbulence and rise in a great roar over the tops of the trees. Then, with a suddenness unheralded, the wind would drop altogether. As Fria was half-way down to the meadow one of these sudden squalls came racing down the valley. It caught Fria unawares. Thrusting up from beneath her, it tipped her into a double wing-over before she knew what was happening. For a second or two she was a panic-struck plaything of the wind which swept her across to the edge of the wood where for a few seconds, wings flicking hard against this new power that assaulted her, Fria was swung and tumbled out of control in the turbulence. The next moment the up-funnelling wind took her under her spread wings in a firm, steady cushion of power that lifted her up to the level of the rookery trees and then above them.

A few rooks saw her. They went up into the wind, rolled and dived untidily towards her, calling angrily to drive her away, knowing there was safety in their numbers, for if she attacked one there were others to confuse her with a blustery attack from an unseen quarter. But Fria was unconcerned with the rooks. Three or four unintentional flicks of her wings took her a hundred feet above the rooks and their wood. Then, as suddenly as it had come, the wind was gone. For a few seconds Fria hung high in the air, hovering on outstretched pinions, kestrel-fashion. In those few seconds a new world came into the scope of her wide-ranging eyes. She could see the Bullay brook running all the way down the valley and disappearing under a road bridge. Beyond that she caught a glimpse of the curving Taw and the hills, oak-and-pine-covered on its far side. She saw houses, farms, hamlets, a train sliding up the valley line and the passage of cars and lorries along the Exeter–Barnstaple road. High above them all, she saw for the first time two broad-winged buzzards circling in the air, turning and wheeling with a slow mastery of the wind. The kestrels she knew and the sparrow-hawks, but these were the first buzzards she had seen. It could have been that she did it from panic, or from a half-understood sense of distant kinship with the hawks, but – for whatever reason – she suddenly uttered in her free state a harsh plaint of *kek-kek-kek*. Then she slid sideways, half-closed her wings and planed down towards her bathing-place. Before she realized it she was going at a speed she had never known before. She overshot the edge of the brook shallows and, instinctively, threw herself up and came out of her dive with wings braking hard against the momentum that still lived in her body. She hovered like a kestrel and then settled clumsily on the brook bank twelve yards from her usual place. It had been her first real experience of the powers of her flight. She sat on the bank for fifteen minutes before she took off in a lull of the wind and flew back to her beam. Nobody at the farm had seen her maneuver.

*   *   *

Mr. Samkin approved of Smiler's essay on Sir

Walter Scott, though he did not agree with his findings. However, Smiler was given permission to borrow the Zeiss binoculars whenever he wished. His need for them was soon to come.

The next evening after Smiler had finished his supper and was rising to go up to his room to study, the Duchess said, "Sit where you are, lad. I want to talk to you for a moment."

"Yes, ma'am." Smiler ran quickly over in his mind all the things he had done at work that day but could think of nothing wrong. The Duchess had shown that she had a sharp eye for slovenly work, and on the few occasions when Smiler had day-dreamed and done a bad job she had told him about it.

The Duchess, guessing what was going through his mind, smiled and shook her head, setting her red curls bouncing (Smiler, prompted by a suggestion Sandra had once made, wondered whether the curls were only a wig) and said, "It's nothing you've done, Samuel. It's what other people have done and, for the sake of peace and quiet here, I want you to know something about it."

"Yes, of course, ma'am."

"You know, lad, that Jimmy hasn't been here for more than a week. That's because I've told him to keep away from this place——"

"What, for good, ma'am?"

"No – until he comes to his senses. We've had a family quarrel, Samuel. I can see his point of view. There's a fire in his blood and anger in his heart. Heeding them could cause him trouble. But that's nothing to saddle you with. All you have to know and say – if anyone asks for him – is that he's got a job travelling with a fair and you don't know which one or where and you don't know when he will be back."

"Yes, ma'am. But he will be back sometime, won't he?"

"I hope so."

Smiler frowned, and then, brightening, said, "Couldn't you look in your crystal ball and find out?"

The Duchess fondled the ears of the Siamese cat Scampi who was sitting in her lap. "One thing I've never done, Samuel, is to ask the crystal ball anything about the future of my kith and kin. It's bad luck."

Up in his room, although it was none of his business, Smiler wondered what the quarrel between the Duchess and Jimmy had been about. He had at the back of his mind a feeling that Jimmy's night excursions to Highford House could have something to do with it. He was pretty sure, however, that Jimmy no longer went there. The little switch broom of hazel twigs had disappeared and, for the last four times when Smiler had been there at night, he had seen no sign of Jimmy and the other man. However, the night before he noticed that the broom was gone, Smiler had discovered something new. No one else but a regular visitor like himself, and then someone with sharp eyes, would have seen it. Some old lengths of roof water piping, which normally lay half-hidden in the long grass, had been collected together and put back in place up the side of the house and fitted to a length of guttering which still remained on one of the lower roof projections. At the bottom of the pipe a disused old iron container from some long ruined wash-house had been dragged into place under the spout. On Smiler's next visit after this discovery the iron container was half full of water that had run down the pipe from the broad, stone roof parapet. Smiler was sure that the farmer who grazed his cattle on the surrounding paddocks and pastures had not fixed up the water supply because in the far corner of the pasture was a modern drinking-trough which was fed from a standpipe linked to the main water supply.

Sitting in his chair and staring at the little clay model of Johnny Pickering on the mantleshelf – the pebble still firmly on its back – Smiler puzzled over all this for a while. Then, with a shrug of his shoulders, he decided that it was no business of his. The Duchess and Jimmy had been good to him. It was not for him to go poking his nose into their quarrels or affairs.

When he went over later that night to make his rounds of the animals in the barn, he paused at the door and shone his torch beam up towards Fria. She was sitting huddled on her perch, well back under the little pent roof.

With an exasperated shake of his head Smiler called up to her, "You stupid old bird – you can't sit up there for the rest of your life."

No movement came from Fria.

*   *   *

March came in that year with an unexpected

warmth and mild breezes from the west. Suddenly the hedgerows were starred with primrose clumps, there was a fresh, metallic greenness to the un-curling fronds of the hart's-tongue ferns, and fragile violets showed their blooms. The fat buds of ash began to swell and there was the smallest drift of green from the hawthorns. There was no rain for two weeks. The Bullay brook dropped to a trickle and the Taw ran low and crystal clear while the estuary at Barnstaple filled with returning salmon waiting for the first spate to let them run the river where even now the kelts from the previous year's spawning season drifted about the pools in which many of them would die before the spate could help take them down to the sea.

On one of these days Smiler spent a day with the local veterinary surgeon – an excursion which had been arranged by the Duchess. The vet. picked him up in his car in the morning and he went round with him on his visits.

The vet. was a cheerful man who liked company especially when it was the kind which was happy to sit and listen to him talk. And talk he did to Smiler as he made his visits to farm and cottage and the small country towns and hamlets. If Smiler had been in any way faint-hearted about his ambition to become a vet. it was a day which would have probably made him change his mind. As it was, at the end of it, his mind was in a whirl but his ambition was still intact. He heard about and saw all sorts of animals and their diseases, about pigs and their enteric complaints and bacterial infections and was told that the pig is basically a very clean animal; he was shown how to handle birds, hens, geese, turkeys and budgerigars; his ears sang with talk about diet deficiencies of proteins and vitamins; he was given the life history of the warble fly that attacks bullocks; he stood by, his eyes missing nothing, while lambs were injected for dysentery, and his head was made to spin with a litany of the diseases of animals – foot-rot, foot-and-mouth, Johne's disease, Scrapie, liver fluke, mange mite, dog fleas, lice, keds and maggot flies – and then surgical details of neutering and spaying cats and the delivery of calves by Caesarean operation. With a twinkle in his eyes and his pipe seldom from his mouth, the vet. inundated Smiler with theory and practical demonstrations all that day as though – rightly proud of his profession – he wanted to test Smiler, to make sure that he really knew what he wanted and knew exactly what it would entail. And Smiler stood up to it because hard work and often dirty work held no fears for him. He knew what he wanted. He wanted to be a vet. and – he was going to become one.

At the end of the day the vet. took him to the bar of the Fox and Hounds Hotel at Eggesford, not far from Bullaybrook Farm, and bought them both quarts of beer (though Smiler would have preferred cider). While they sat drinking it, the vet. said, "Well, Samuel – that's just one day. And not ended yet. There'll be more waiting for me at the surgery. Think you can take it?"

"Oh, I'm sure I can, sir."

The vet. eyed him over his tankard and said,

"Ay, I think you can. You've got a good pair of hands and a strong stomach. You've a long way to go, but you've all the time in the world before you. If ever you want any help come and see me."

That evening Smiler wrote in his diary:

Spent the whole day with Mr. Rhodes. I think the Duchess must have told him to rub my nose in it – and didn't he by half! But it don't make no difference. Bother – any. I'm going to be a vet. The beer at the Fox and Hounds was good. I think I could get to like it as much as cider. Letter today from Laura. Only two mingy pages and most of that about somebody's funeral she went to. Fria just the same.

5

↜ Some Hard Lessons to Learn ↝

The mild weather hastened Spring to the Taw
valley. While Smiler went on with his work at the
farm and his studies with Mr. Samkin – who now
had Smiler groaning because he was insisting that
he should learn some Latin and was hinting that
very soon Smiler would have to take a proper
series of correspondence courses with some educa-
tional institution so that he could prepare for his
first examinations – things were happening in other
places which would eventually shape Smiler's
destiny.

In Bristol Albert and Ethel had received a letter
from Smiler's father by air mail from Australia.
The relevant part of the letter which concerned
Smiler read:

> I don't know what the police and the shipping
> company have been playing at in not letting me
> know what's been going on. They say they've
> sent me stuff but I never got it. Anyway, that's
> all water under the bridge and I can't get back
> yet to do anything about it. There's a dock strike
> out here and we're stuck till the lads decide to
> unload us – and could you see the company
> flying me home? Not B. likely.
>
> But that don't worry me because I know my
> Samuel M. You just give him the letter what

I'm enclosing and he'll know what he's got to do. But I don't want you or Ethel to do or say anything about this to anyone, mind, until Samuel M. gets the letter.

Ethel, who was sitting holding the sealed letter to Smiler while Albert read to her, made a sour face and said, "Just like him. Putting it all on to somebody else. Out of sight, out of mind."

Albert gave an inward sigh and said mildly, "Well, dear, it isn't quite like that. What else could he do? And my bet is that he's given Smiler some sound advice."

"That Smiler – the trouble he's caused."

"Not to us, dear. To the police, maybe – but then they're paid for it."

Ethel held up the letter gingerly by one corner as though it might contain poison and said, "Well – and what about this? We get letters from him – but no address and postmarked all over the place. How we goin' to get this to him?"

Albert sighed again, audibly this time, and said, "I don't know. But I'll find a way." He rose and took the letter from his wife. Looking round the prim front parlour where he was not allowed to smoke and always had to wear his carpet slippers, he went on, "I'll just go out to me workshop and think it over for an hour. Something'll come to me."

After half an hour contentedly smoking in his workshop, nothing had come to Albert. But he was not downhearted because Albert was a philosopher and he knew that most problems had a way – if you waited long enough – of solving themselves. He only hoped that this one would not be so long in coming that it would be too late for Smiler to take whatever advice his father was giving. He locked the letter away in his little workshop desk for safety. Ethel, he knew, had the curiosity of a jackdaw. She was well capable of steaming the letter open and reading it.

In Bristol, too, Johnny Pickering was becoming a little frightened and puzzled. He was getting letters recently from all over the place – Southampton, London, Manchester, Glasgow, Durham – and seldom a week passed without one dropping on to the front door-mat.

They were all printed in ink in the same hand without address or signature and there was never more than one sentence in them. The first five had read:

CONFESSION IS GOOD FOR THE SOUL
YOU DID IT AND THE INNOCENT SUF-
FERED
OWN UP AND AVOID BAD LUCK
NOTHING WILL GO RIGHT UNTIL YOU
ARE RIGHT WITH YOURSELF
THE BLACK HAND IS OVER YOU AND
THE GREEN EYES ARE WATCHING
ONLY THREE MORE WARNINGS BEFORE
FATE STRIKES

At first Johnny Pickering had tried to take no notice of the letters. But he could not keep it up. Things suddenly *did* seem to have started to go wrong with him. He slipped on the pavement and badly twisted his ankle. His girl friend told him she wanted no more to do with him and found herself another boy. He began to get in trouble at work breaking things in the china shop where he was employed as a counter assistant. He knew perfectly well what all the letters were about and he thought they came from Smiler. But he couldn't work out how Smiler could be dodging about all over England posting them. He said nothing to his parents, but his slowly changing manner, making him irritable and rude, often brought him a smart backhander from his father. There were times when he heartily wished he had never stolen the old lady's handbag and put the blame on Smiler.

And while Albert pondered what to do about Smiler's letter and Johnny Pickering swore, less and less convincingly, that he was never going to be daft enough to go and make a clean breast of things to the police, Smiler was facing his own problems; some minor – like the way Sandra still hung around and foisted her company on him whenever she could; and one major – his disquiet over Fria who still sat on her beam and did little more than fly down to the shallows most days to bathe and was quite content to take food from the loft ledge.

He talked his major problem over one day with Mr. Samkin who had become, in a way, more of a confidant for him than the Duchess who seemed to go about the farm now preoccupied and – Smiler guessed – clearly worrying about her rift with Jimmy.

Mr. Samkin said, "There's nothing you can do but have patience, Samuel. In the wild state Fria would have been taught everything by her parents. Animals have to be taught. But she was taken before all that could happen. Now, if she wants to live free, she's got to learn everything herself. Imagine if you woke up one day on a Pacific island beach – ten years old, and you couldn't speak, knew no language, had never climbed a tree or peeled a banana, couldn't swim. How would you feel?"

"Pretty lost."

"Well, that's Fria. She's pretty lost. But she's got food and water and shelter of a kind. No matter what kind of spirit she's got she's sensible enough to stay where she is. Would you take it on yourself to drive her away deliberately? To cut off her food supply?"

"I couldn't, sir."

Mr. Samkin smiled gently. "Of course not. But something might. Some accident. If on your desert island you slipped and fell into the sea you'd make an instinctive effort to swim. If it came off – you'd have survived. If you were hungry you'd find yourself picking some fruit or other and trying it. If you didn't like its taste you'd spit it out. If you liked it you'd eat it. Self-education forced on man or beast has only two ends – survival or death. Fria isn't going to move from the safety of her beam until something too powerful for her to resist makes her."

"And then she might die, sir."

Mr. Samkin nodded gravely. "The odds are she

95

will, Samuel. There's no sentiment in Mother Nature."

*   *   *

Two days later the mild weather broke. The westerly breezes died and the wind moved round to the north-east. There was a night of bitter, sharp frost and the next day the wind freshened and with it came a hard, cold rain which swept down into the Taw valley in rolling, biting clouds and came racing up the Bullay brook in veil after veil of stinging, blinding squalls. In no time at all the woods and fields ran with water and the brook rose a foot before mid-day, swirling riverwards now in a brown flood carrying winter debris and litter with it. Birds and beasts hugged their shelters. The rooks clung to their wood and were tossed and drenched on their nests, sitting close to the first eggs which had been laid. In the fields the bullocks and sheep moved to sheltered corners and turned their backs on the icy downpour. In the farm-yard the only animals who enjoyed themselves were the few ducks the Duchess kept. They puddled about over the flooded cobbles and shovelled and dabbled their bills in the mud around the banks of the swollen shallows where Fria bathed.

Fria had no temptation that day to bathe. She sat on her beam, well back under the little pent roof and faced the cold onslaught of rain. Had she been an entirely wild peregrine she would have crept into the shelter of some small cliff crevice or tree hole and hidden from the weather. She

96

sat there all day until just before the light began to go. There was a lull in the cold rainstorms and she flew down to the loft ledge and ate, tearing at a small rabbit which Smiler had left for her. Over the months she had learned slowly and awkwardly now how to pluck and find the breasts of the pigeons she was given and how to tear at the skin of rabbits and find her way to the succulent flesh of flanks and hindquarters.

Her meal done, she flew back to her beam and watched the evening darkness flood the valley while the renewed rain, heavier than before, slashed down as though it meant to drown the world. The brook was so swollen with the run-offs from the valley that it had come up four feet in a fast storm spate, a coffee-coloured foam and scud-topped torrent that beat high against the arch of the small stone road-bridge and was already spreading over the lower parts of the pasture and, within an hour, was to be over the road by the bridge.

When Smiler went out late that night to visit the barn, the rain battered against his storm jacket and the yard water swilled around his gum-boots. He flicked his torch up to Fria and saw her huddled tight back against the barn wall into which the beam was set. For a moment or two he was tempted to creep up quietly into the loft and make a grab for her and put her back into the shelter of her cage, but it was a thought that died almost before it was born. In the darkness and rain he was sure to make a muff of it and, anyway, he knew that Fria would not be sleeping. She would

97

be alert to any noise or movement from the loft. He did his round of the barn, came back across the flooded yard to check the stable doors and then went off to bed.

He lay in bed, reading and listening to the rain beat at his window, and finally he slept.

Outside Fria knew no sleep. She knew only the darkness peopled by darker shapes and the noise of the rain and the higher, steadier noise of the spate-filled brook racing away towards the Taw.

An hour before first morning-light the weather changed. The steady downpour eased off, sometimes stopped for a few minutes, and then abruptly what wind there was backed to the north-west and began to strengthen. Within half an hour it was roaring straight in from the sea and the long reaches of the Atlantic, thundering over miles of countryside and howling down into the valley from the far slope in a full gale that stripped dead branches from trees, seized anything that was loose and tossed it into the air, plucked slates from roofs and tore great patches in the old thatch of cottages. It came now not in one long steady pulse of moving, turbulent air, but in great gusty spasms that would follow a lull, and sometimes – because of the vagaries of the land over which it poured – it would change direction suddenly.

Her body plumage tightened down against its force, her eyes half closed as she faced the wind, Fria clung to her beam and there was a strength now in her legs and talons that held her firm against the sudden vortices and vigorous up-draughts that swirled against the little pent roof above her. Now from this side, now from that, now from above and now from below, the violent, invisible tide assaulted Fria, and she held her place and would have gone on holding her place had it not been for the unexpected.

The loft door which was open behind her was held in place by a small bar on its rear side which was hooked into a stout staple which had been driven into one of the cross-beams of the roof timbers that straddled the inside of the loft. The hook and staple were strong, but the wood of the cross-beam, though its heart was a solid core of oak, had an outer lay of ancient wood which had been bored and tunnelled by woodworm. Each time the wind roared into the loft and then was drawn back like a violently receding wave, the suction wrenched at the loft door, trying to draw it shut. And each time the door jerked under the vacuum pull of the wind the staple worked a little looser.

Finally, as the first grey light of dawn struggled through the curtains of wind-driven rain, the gale smashed against the face of the barn, shaking its roof and timbers, soared upwards, howled around the loft and then was drawn back in a fierce out-going eddy, violent with turbulence and power. The staple was pulled from its beam and the loft door was sucked back with a speed and savagery that would have killed anything which barred its path. The door crashed into its frame, shattering and bursting it outwards. Timbers and woodwork flew out into the air and the door, torn from its hinges, followed on the heels of an explosion of sound like a crack of thunder. The wind took the door, lifted it, and sent it slicing high through the air as though it had been a sheet of paper. (It was found two days later by Bob and Bill in a field of young wheat at the top of the hill road at the brow of the valley.)

And with the door went Fria.

The great crash of the door slamming into and through its frame six inches below and behind her was like the report of a cannon being fired close to her. She jumped with fear on her beam and half spread her wings in panic. The wind took her. Wings wide, her long tail-feathers spread, the wind sucked her up like a straw and she was whipped across the face of the barn and then swung round its corner. As though the gale were some living, malicious personality treating her like a new toy in its old, old game, it flung her skywards on a great updraught of eddying and coiling currents of air. She went up five hundred feet in a few seconds and, as she went, she was pitched and somersaulted out of control.

A fully mature and experienced peregrine with all its powers could have ridden the wind and would have known better than to fight the impossible. A fully mature and experienced peregrine would never voluntarily have put to flight in such a wind and – if caught in one – would have gone to ground, to eyrie or to shelter as quickly as it could along the line of least resistance, stooping with the wind's direction and flattening its line of dive long before sanctuary was too dangerously near.

Fria had no such wisdom. In a panic she fought the air with her wings, and the wind took the resistance she gave and flipped her over and upwards in a ragged series of back-somersaults. When Fria righted herself she was a thousand feet above ground, though she could see little of it in the pale morning light because of the scuds of driving rain that charged across the land in rolling onslaughts.

Fria wailed with panic, caught sight of the barn far below her, and automatically, since it represented shelter, half rolled, closed her wings and began to dive towards it as she had once come down from high above the rookery to her bathing-place. The maneuver did her no good at all. The power of the wind, rising almost vertically beneath her, held her where she was for a moment and then lifted her and rolled her over and over. She was swung up another five hundred feet, and the howling and roaring of the wind around her filled her mind with a greater panic.

For some seconds the gale threw her about the sky in its updraught and then spewed her out of its ascending vortex into the gale-force main stream of its south-easterly path. There, from luck, chance, or some dim ancestral bodily memory that informed her muscles and wings, she found herself doing the right thing. With three-quarter-closed wings, her tail feathers tight in a narrow wedge shape, her head lowered, she found herself going downwind fast and slowly losing height.

Her panic eased a little with the discovery, and

she leaned on the back of the wind, increased her glide to a faster dive, and came down through the rain and saw the earth coming up to her fast. She saw trees, woods, fields, the dark shine of a flooded river and then, away to her right, the rain-darkened stonework of a building that reminded her of the barns and Bullaybrook Farm.

Full of fear, but calmer now that she was under some sort of control, Fria leaned across the wind and wore down the gale in a fast, curving arc and – because she wanted to do it – her natural flight powers obeyed her and she began to flatten her descent though she did not slacken it much. She flashed dangerously low across the tossing, waving tops of a wide expanse of fir plantation, dropped below its far edge into shelter from the gale, and found herself heading fast for the sprawling bulk of the grey stone building she had seen. She curved across the building ten feet above it and, now in some primitive control of herself, threw up sharply and then had to fight the upsurging momentum of her own body with rapid brake-beats of her wings. A few seconds later she landed clumsily in tall grasses fifty yards from the building. She sat, hidden in the wet grasses, the rain beating down on her. She sat, half crouched, her wings half spread, the rain striking down at them, and she wailed three or four times like a lonely, unhappy, lost child. But as with an un-tutored, immature child one emotion moves on erratic impulse rapidly to another, Fria felt sudden anger in herself. Her wailing ceased. At this moment, since her eyes never missed any movement, she saw something stir in the tall grasses a couple of feet from her.

It was a little shrew that had been flooded out of its earth burrow. Fria jumped forward and angrily grabbed at it with her beak. Her powerful mandibles clamped across its tiny neck and killed it. For a moment Fria sat with it in her beak. Then with a toss of her head she jerked it from her.

*　　*　　*

Smiler was full of dismay when he discovered that Fria had gone. The manner of her going was no mystery to him or to Bob and Bill.

"That old door, Sammy, must have come out like a shell from a gun. But if she was up on the beam it wouldn't have hit her," said Bill. "Don't you worry. She'll be back when she gets hungry."

But Smiler was far from content with that. Fria was not a homing pigeon. The gale could have blown her miles away, and the gale was still blowing. She might, perhaps, have been injured, broken a wing or something, and be somewhere in the nearby woods and fields. He decided that he just had to try and find her. If she were uninjured and wanted to stay free . . . well, that was all right with him. But if she were injured . . . well, then he had a duty to try and find her.

That day was a Saturday and he finished work at mid-day. He ate a hurried lunch and then cycled up to Mr. Samkin and borrowed his binoculars. From then until the light went he spent his time cycling around the countryside and along the paths in the Forestry Commission plantations looking for Fria. The wind was still blowing hard, but the rain had now slackened to occasional fierce showers.

Smiler went to every high point he could think of and searched the sky and then the countryside for a sign of the falcon. But he had no luck. He went to Highford House. He sat there for half an hour, sweeping his glasses round and round. But there was no sign of Fria. At least no sign that he could recognize, though he passed one as he left the place by way of the overgrown garden. The limp, bedraggled mole-grey body of a dead shrew lay in the grass. And he would have been surprised – and delighted – if he could have known that Fria was watching him as he moved about the building and the garden.

Fria recognized him. But that was all. She was no familiar dog or cat to come to him, eager to make herself known. She sat where she was and watched him go. Neither hunger nor thirst had worried her yet, but there was a difference in her which now informed all her movements and emotions. She had ridden the gale. The memory of her panic had gone but not, probably, the memory of the way she had finally used the wind to achieve sanctuary of a kind. Like all creatures, once she had done something the repetition of the act presented no fears. She learned by doing; and the more often a thing was done the more adept a creature became at it. Nature is a rough teacher, but her lessons stick, or else. . . .

Smiler cycled back to the farm with a long face

and it was made longer when the Duchess reminded him that Sandra was coming to dinner – a return invitation which the Duchess had insisted he make because he had been to Sandra's party. Smiler groaned, and groaned again when the Duchess said, "And what's more, you've only got half an hour to bath and change before she comes. And, of course –" she grinned and reached out and pulled his snub nose – "you'll walk her home in the dark afterwards like a perfect gentleman. And you needn't think you're being untrue to that Laura of yours. She's not sitting at home every night doing her knitting and mooning about you. Now get off with you – and don't fuss about that bird. God's hand is large and it casts a wide shadow over the world."

"Who said that?" asked Smiler.

"Well, I did of course. I just said it."

"Oh, I thought it was a quotation."

"Well, thank you, Sammy. But remember – there's no wisdom in any book which wasn't first spoken by someone."

Smiler paused at the door and with a grin said, "Do I really have to walk her home?" Then he ducked out of the doorway to avoid a cushion being thrown at him. The Duchess went off into the kitchen chuckling to herself. But once she was alone and the thought of Smiler's falcon came back to her her face grew serious. She was remembering something Jimmy had said before she had told him not to stay at the farm any longer.

"If freedom is your right, then it's better to die than let any man take it from you. And, if needs be, it's better to be hunted all your life than live in a cage."

That evening was not the ordeal which Smiler had thought it might be. Sandra looked very nice in a blue dress which contrasted with her fair complexion and blonde hair. It was curious, Smiler decided, how once you got used to something you almost stopped noticing it, like the slight prominence of her aquiline nose. In fact, too, the word aquiline pleased him because he had only recently discovered it in his reading and – following Mr. Samkin's instructions never to pass a new word without looking it up in the dictionary – he knew that it came from the word *aquila* – the golden eagle. Hooked like an eagle's beak . . . "Well, be fair, Samuel M.," he told himself, "it wasn't really as bad as that."

Over dinner the Duchess told them tales of her circus life and how she had been born in a horse-drawn caravan in a field somewhere on the south side of Dartmoor. When she was old enough she had worked with her mother selling the wooden clothes-pegs her father and brothers made from door to door, and posies of spring and summer flowers, until the day had come when she was a young woman and had met her husband, the Duke. She had gone into the circus with him and started her career as a fortune teller. But after he had died her heart had turned from the circus and, with the money she had saved, she had bought Bullaybrook Farm and retired.

When dinner was over they played three-handed cards and put records on the player, though neither

Sandra nor Smiler thought much of the records because they were donkey's years old. Then the old piano was opened up and Smiler, who in the past months had spent a lot of time on it and, having a good ear, had taught himself to play quite well, gave them some of the songs they knew and others that he had learnt from his father. While he played one of his father's favourites, *The Streams of Lovely Nancy*, he wondered where his father was at that moment and how long it would be before he saw him and between them they could get all his troubles sorted out so that he could go full steam ahead with his ambition to be a vet.

Walking Sandra back up the hill to her village afterwards it was very dark and half-way up the hill Sandra stumbled and took his arm to keep her balance. And then she kept her hand on his arm and, somehow, a little later Smiler found that she was holding his hand. He felt very embarrassed about it but clearly Sandra did not consider it anything strange.

She said, "If you're going to do all this studying why don't you try to be a doctor? After all that's a much better thing than spending your time with dirty old animals and birds."

Smiler said indignantly, "Animals and birds aren't dirty – not if people keep them properly. And, anyway, being a vet. is harder than being a doctor. After all, people can tell a doctor where they've got their pains and aches and, if he's done his stuff, well, he ought to know how to treat them. But animals can't speak. You've got to . . . well, sort of get into their minds for them and find out what's wrong sometimes."

Sandra said, "You've always got an answer, haven't you?" And then, going off at a tangent, she went on, "I had a good look tonight, and you know, I don't think that is a wig the Duchess wears. It's her own hair. But why does she wear it in those tight little curls?"

"If you're so interested – why didn't you ask her?"

At the front door of Sandra's house, she paused in the darkness before going in and said very politely, "Well, thank you very much, Sammy, for a very pleasant evening."

"Thank you for coming."

Sandra laughed and said, "And now, if you want to, you can kiss me goodnight."

Startled, Smiler blurted out, "Good Lord, I couldn't do that!"

Sandra giggled. "Why not?"

"Well . . . well, you don't. You don't kiss people unless you love them."

"And you don't love me?" asked Sandra teasingly.

"Of course I don't."

"Who do you love then?"

"That's none of your business."

"I don't care if it isn't. And, anyway, I kiss people because I like them and they've been nice to me. So –" She leaned forward and gave him a smacking great kiss on the cheek and nearly poked his left eye out with her nose.

Smiler turned and ran until he was out of the

village. When he slowed up and began the walk back down the hill, he thought, "Gosh, girls . . . you have to be on your toes all the time with them, or you're in trouble."

Half-way down the hill he had further proof of this which he entered at the end of his diary that night. The diary entry finished:

. . . but I'm sure Fria can't have gone very far. I'm going to spend all day tomorrow looking for her. If she's lodged up somewhere I could bring food to her.

Trouble tonight with that Sandra. I think she only does it to get me all muddled up. Which is what it does what with worrying about Fria and thinking about what Laura would say. Though you never know with her. She might just laugh her head off. And to make matters worse that boy friend of hers (Sandra's) must have been hanging around because he stopped me on the hill coming back and told me what he would do if I didn't keep away from Sandra. I told him he could keep his old Sandra. And then he got nasty so – him being bigger than me – I said to put his head in a bucket and ran for home.

Being a vet. is much more difficult than being a doctor.

I think it could have been Trevor Green that caused all the trouble in the barn and let Fria free. The pebble is still on Johnny P's shoulders. Can't see how it can ever fall off.

'And so to bed' – Samuel Pepys Miles!!

6

∽ *First Steps Towards Freedom* ∽

Smiler had an early breakfast the next morning,
did his chores around the barns and the yard, and
then spent the rest of the daylight hours searching
for Fria. At times, when he met farm workers and
the country people he had now come to know, it
was a temptation to ask them if they had seen the
falcon. But he held back from doing so because he
knew how fast the news would travel round, and
that would alert trigger-happy folk who just shot
at anything that moved.

The gale had dropped now to a steady blow
from the north-east, driving great banks of high
cumulus clouds across a pale-blue sky. Now and
again there would be a fierce, brief shower. The
Taw and its tributary streams were running high and
some of the valley fields were flooded with the spate.

Smiler cycled for miles to every vantage point
he could think of and others that he picked off the
one-inch-to-the-mile ordnance survey map he had
bought of the district. He got wet and he got dry
again, and he got tired and he got hungry. At
lunchtime he called at the Fox and Hounds hotel
bar and had a pint of cider and a plate of sandwiches. The barman was a jolly man with dark
hair and long sideburns and wore a red waistcoat.
As he served Smiler, he said, "The Duchess's
nephew, ain't you?" When Smiler nodded, the

barman grinned, thrust out his right hand, and said with a wink, "Here you are then, tell me fortune. Shall I win the football pools next week?"

Smiler laughed, but as he ate his lunch the idea came to him that if he didn't find Fria maybe the Duchess could look in her crystal ball and get some information – though he had to admit that it was a slim hope.

For the rest of the afternoon Smiler searched, using Mr. Samkin's binoculars and carefully putting them back in their case when he had finished each time. He saw plenty of birds. There were lapwings still flocking on the high fields, mallard, widgeon and teal flighting along the flooded meadows, and once a skein of geese moving high in a wavering line northwards against the wind. Buzzard pairs wheeled and soared over the dark pine woods, swans winged heavily up the river and kestrels hovered over the brown heather and dead bracken clumps in the forestry clearings. But Smiler saw no sign of Fria. But once, high, high up, two or three thousand feet, he guessed, he picked out to the north a small, dark crescent shape which was gone quickly into the blazing eye of the sun as a racing cloud-patch uncovered it briefly. It was a peregrine, Smiler was sure, but he couldn't believe that it was Fria, riding so high and so confidently. A few seconds' observation of the bird marked it as one that had been born to freedom and wore its liberty and powers untouched by any taint of captivity. Smiler was right, for the peregrine he briefly saw was a tiercel from the cliffs of Blackstone Point beyond Ilfracombe.

With his glasses Smiler scanned the edges of woods and the clumps of isolated elms and oaks, seeking for the still graven shape of Fria perched on some high branch or merged against some tree-trunk. All he saw was the movement of wood pigeons and ring-doves and the black scattering of rooks and crows. Knowing that Fria was used to barns and farm buildings, he searched around field barns and hay stores and the roofs of the farmhouses – all without success. It was this knowledge that Fria might have chosen some building for shelter that took him with only half an hour of daylight left to Highford House, debating in his mind whether if he did not find Fria today – a Sunday – he could dare ask the Duchess for the next day off to go on with his search and promise to work the following Sunday to make it up. If it had been Jimmy Jago he had had to ask he knew that permission would have been given. But there was no Jimmy around now, and the Duchess had a funny little streak about jobs being done when they should be done. And, anyway, in his heart he felt that the Duchess had already given Fria up as lost for good.

He went all over Highford House and the ruined buildings around it. He searched inside the red brick tower, climbing as high as he dared until he met a great gap in the spiralling stone stairway. There was no sign of Fria.

Despondently Smiler gave up the search and went back to where he had left his bicycle in the wild rhododendron shrubbery at the back of the house. He cycled away down the wet, gravelly, moss-patched old driveway. As he went a jay shrieked suddenly at him from a branch as though in derision.

*   *   *

Fria watched him go. She was lodged within a foot of the top of the red brick tower. Here, there had long ago been a fall of bricks from the curved side of the tower which had made a recess about two feet high and three feet wide. The recess ran back through the masonry to the inner wall of the tower, forming a shelf which was protected from the weather. Two bricks had fallen inwards from the rear wall making a hole through which one could look down into the well of the tower past a small section of stone stairway that still survived to the great gap that reached far below to the commencement of the stairs again. On the outside of the tower, ivy had grown up, rooted in the bricks twelve feet below. It covered one side of the recess and formed a leafy screen. Above the recess, stonecrop had taken root and formed pale green pads along an ornamental ridge. From the tower-top – where the seed had years ago been excreted by a thrush – a trail of bramble, touched now with new leaf spurs, cascaded downwards in a ragged sweep.

From the ground it was almost impossible to see that the tower-top held Fria's recess. But Fria, although she sat well back, could see everything that moved below. She had seen Smiler come and now she watched him go and, because she associated him with food and she was hungry, there had been a moment before his going when she had almost wailed from the sudden sharpness of the association twisting physically inside her. Hunger she had, but not thirst. Twice that day she had taken off into the steady wind and flown to the tower-top where the rains had formed puddles in the warped and dented hollows of the old lead roof sheeting that still remained there. And twice that day she had moved off in a slow, circular flight, low down, skirting around Highford House itself, beating with steady wing-flicks across the bullock pasture and then coming back in a fast rising flight to the tower recess. Flight was not now the panic-maker it had been. The wind was firm, a steady blow which she mastered and used easily so long as she was not called upon to perform any unexpected or skilful maneuver. On her second, non-drinking flight, she had dropped to the grass where she had killed the shrew. Mice and shrews she had eaten before and hunger spurred her search for this shrew. The shrew had gone, its limp body long ago seen by a crow and carried away.

If Smiler had stayed another ten minutes he might have found Fria, for now, as he cycled down the drive a half a mile away, she suddenly wailed and moved forward to the edge of the recess. In the dying light she launched herself easily and flapped slowly across the abandoned, ruined gardens, moving more like an owl than a peregrine. She dropped her head and searched the ground beneath her. Even in the fading light, her great eyes – so big that if a man's were in the same proportion to his body size they would have been three inches wide – missed nothing. She saw a pale cinnamon moth climbing a dead willow-herb stalk, saw the slight heave of the ground where a mole worked unseen, and the slow draw of a dead leaf where a worm pulled it down into its tunnel. She was hungry, and hunger is the great dictator. A field-mouse poked its nose from under a rain-flattened patch of long-dead wild geranium. Fria saw the fine tremble of its whiskers, the small skin-movement as it creased its snout and flicked its eyes from side to side. Because the mouse meant food to her and she wanted it she slid up into the air a few feet. Her muscles were schooled by the desire in her to hang above the rodent. She hung on poised wings, her long primaries just trembling, the narrow wedge of her tail suddenly spread wide as she hovered like a kestrel. She did what many of her wild kin often did from time to time. Sometimes, indeed, they hovered, sharing the same field or orchard with a kestrel for at certain times of the year there was a strange amity between the two species.

The mouse moved out from its shelter and ran in jerky, staccato movements between the tall grasses. Fria moved, following it, hovering still. Then, the excitement in her for food so strong, she raised her wings and dropped to the grass, thrusting out her legs, talons open to grasp the mouse. The mouse leapt away and scuttled to the safety of the root tangle of an old crab-apple tree. Fria, missing the mouse, hit the ground lightly but clumsily. She sat on the grass, folded her long wings over her tail, preened irritably at her slate-streaked pale breast and then wailed gently. After a few moments she jumped lightly into the air and began to quarter across the ground between the tower and the ruined house, hovering and watching the ground and then sliding a few yards to another vantage position. But nothing moved on the ground, and a steady rain shower, heavy, and pounding the ground with fat drops, blackened the sky and drove the last of the light from the day.

Fria winged over gently and beat up to her recess. She shook the water from her plumage and then walked to the back of the recess and began to dress and preen her feathers. The night settled around her, steady with the noise of creaking branches and the whisper of the ivy leaves that screened part of the recess opening. Fria slept, forgetting her hunger and her anger. An hour later a barn owl that lived in a dead oak a mile away came drifting over the abandoned garden and took the field mouse which Fria had missed.

*　　*　　*

The next morning in Bristol a letter arrived for Johnny Pickering before he went off to work. Inside was the familiar sheet of paper and on it was written: THERE IS ONLY ONE WAY TO AVOID THE DARK DAYS AHEAD.

His father, sitting across the table from him, saw the paper in his hand and said, "What's that, then?"

In surly tones Johnny Pickering said, "Never you mind. It's my business."

His father, bad-tempered and with a headache from too much beer the previous night, leaned across the table quickly and gave him a smack on the head which sent Johnny from his chair to the floor.

"Add that to it, then," said his father.

It was a good beginning to the week, thought Johnny as he cycled to work. But, anyway, he was used to taking the odd clout from his father and he certainly wasn't going to let the letters upset him. Yet, tell himself what he may, he *was* upset by them. Knowing what he did about Smiler he couldn't see them as being his style. Somebody else was doing it. Suddenly the alarming thought struck him that maybe the police suspected him and someone at the station was trying to frighten him into telling the truth. He was so absorbed by this thought that when a small van drew up rather sharply ahead of him, although he braked hard and in reasonable time, his front wheel hit the back of the van and was too much buckled for him to ride it. As he dragged his bicycle to the pavement he remembered the words in one of the letters: NOTHING WILL GO RIGHT UNTIL YOU ARE RIGHT WITH YOURSELF.

*　　*　　*

And at the breakfast table at Albert and Ethel's house, Ethel, in her dressing-gown and with her hair in curlers (a sight which Albert could not bear but had to), said "Well, have you decided yet what to do about that letter for Smiler?"

117

"No, I haven't."

"But you've got to. It's important."

"Well, what do you want me to do? Put an advert in all the papers all over the country? Have an S.O.S. broadcast on the radio? *Will Samuel Miles, wanted by the police, please contact his brother-in-law where he will hear of something to his advantage.* I don't think. Not with a copper waiting on the doorstep."

"Oh, sarky, aren't we, this morning," said Ethel.

"Sorry, luv," said Albert, who was really a nice-natured man. Monday morning was always bad for him because he was suffering from Sunday when he was made to go to chapel twice a day and tidy up and dig in the small garden which he hated and then no television in the evening because Ethel didn't hold with it on a Sunday.

"Well, something's got to be done," said Ethel practically. "Nobody's going to turn up out of the blue, ringing our doorbell to tell us where he's hidden himself."

"I suppose not," said Albert.

*   *   *

And on that Monday morning a prisoner at Princetown Gaol was marched out with a working party under the guard of warders to do quarrying on the moor close to the prison.

He was a tall, solidly built man in his forties. He had short, sandy hair, blue eyes, and a tanned craggy face creased with good-humoured lines. Cheerfulness was second nature to him and self-reliance went with it. Bitterness he had known once but it had been burned from him.

He looked up at the rain-washed sky and, because he had always lived an open-air life, sensed at once the quarter the wind was in, knew from the look of the day whether it would shift and what changes might come. On this morning he knew for sure that the likelihood of there being a sudden, cloaking Dartmoor mist was something he wouldn't bet a farthing on.

He walked along in the ranks of prisoners and watched the long slopes of the moor, caught the white-barred flick of a snipe's wings as it rose from a ditch, and half-whistled, half-hummed a tune to himself. The man at his side – one of the trusty few who knew his secret – winked at him and said from the side of his mouth, "No excursion ticket for sale today, Maxie."

Maxie winked back and grinned. Life was long, life was earnest, and patience was a good thing – but best of all, he told himself, was faith. His day would come. The mist would come and all he would need would be a hundred yards start, and he would be away towards the high tors he knew like the back of his hand, and streaking like a hare for freedom. And why shouldn't he? A man had to do what his heart and his nature told him was just. But justice was one thing and the law was another. He grinned to himself and then, seeing a wood pigeon in flight across the road ahead, he fell to thinking of the time when he had been a very young man and had kept pigeons . . . brown and white and black and white West of England tumblers that fell through the sky in a madness of whirling wings and somersaults that cut the air with a sound like tearing calico . . . the beauties, the little beauties. . . .

*　　*　　*

And that morning Smiler sat at breakfast without much appetite. The Duchess, with Scampi on her lap, eyed him over the table and knew exactly what his trouble was and, because she was a good-hearted woman, though easily severe when she felt it was wise, she said, "If you square it with Bob and Bill and work all day next Saturday, you can take today off to look for that blessed Fria of yours."

"Oh, thank you very much, ma'am. I would like to do that."

Smiler had no trouble arranging things with Bill and Bob because more than once he had done them good turns. So once more he set off on his bicycle with his map and his glasses, and as he rode along he settled his plan of campaign if he should be lucky enough to find Fria. He didn't want to capture her. All he wanted was to know where she was and then keep an eye on her. She was free now and he had a good idea that hunger would force her to find some kind of food for herself, even if she had to scavenge for it. All he wanted was to be on hand while she learnt to look after herself and – if it was a slow process – to be able to leave her a dead rabbit or wood pigeon now and then to keep her going. On no account, he told himself, was he

120

going to take over full provisioning because that would be a mistaken kindness. Fate had set her free and now – if she still survived – she would have to learn the hard lessons of a life of liberty for herself. If she had been brought up naturally in her parents' eyrie, they would have done the teaching for her. He knew, for instance, from his reading, that the great skill of a peregrine stooping vertically from hundreds of feet on to its flying prey, slashing past it and killing it with the rear talons of one or both feet was something which had to be taught by the parents. Maybe, if Fria survived long enough, she would learn that great maneuver of speed and timing for herself.

As he rode through the countryside, stopping now and then to sweep the landscape with his glasses, Fria was already learning some lessons for herself.

She woke at first light. In the grey dawn she flew up to the tower-roof and drank some water. The rains had gone, but the sky was overcast with low, heavy clouds that broke now and then to show patches of blue sky from which a watery sun briefly bathed the land in its light. Her thirst satisfied, Fria went back to her recess. Hunger was a tightening knot inside her. On the bricked face of the recess a brief movement caught her eye. It was a small spider which had crept to the mouth of a funnel-shaped web it had made in a crack between the bricks. Its movement brought a quick reflex action from Fria. She stabbed at it with her beak, caught, and swallowed it. She moved around the recess and found another spider which she caught and ate. The acts of catching and eating stimulated her. Within the next half hour she had taken four wood lice that had moved from under the dead ivy leaves which littered one corner of the recess. The amount of food was negligible and the taste faintly disagreeable. Having, for the moment, exhausted the insect life of her recess, she walked to the edge and looked down into the garden. After a few moments she flew down and settled in the damp, overgrown tangle of grasses and dead bracken. She began to stalk slowly through this miniature jungle, her eyes alert for any movement. She took a worm that writhed, half-dead, at the edge of a puddle and ate it. She spent an hour scavenging through the wild garden, took three more worms, four spiders, and a fat dor-beetle. The knot of hunger in her slackened a little, but not enough to come anywhere near satisfying her. Because she was a bird of quick temperament the slow process of feeding irritated her to the point where once or twice she gave an angry call . . . *yek-yek-yek*.

She launched herself and flew up twenty feet and began to quarter the ground, hovering like a kestrel. Her move into the air sent a thrush that was cracking a snail on a loose masonry slab by the old house flying fast and low into the cover of a thicket of dead old man's beard which trailed in a tangled mantle over a stunted hawthorn bush. Fria, alert and reflexes working sharply, went after it like a sparrow-hawk. But she was far too slow and the thrush found sanctuary easily. Fria soared up a little at the end of her chase and hovered briefly over the hawthorn and its creeper tangle. A pair of magpies coming over the roofless house saw her, and recognized the menace of her shape and poise, sharp-tipped wings flicking, tapping at the air as though they quivered in some fine ecstasy. They dived for the cover of the dark labyrinths of the overgrown rhododendrons by the old driveway.

Fria beat up to the top of the tower and settled there above her recess. She sat there for ten minutes slowly bobbing her head up and down irritably as though she were giving herself a good talking to. She saw the movement of dozens of birds in the great arc of her vision, caught the black and white fidgeting of a dipper on a post down by the flooded river and, once, the streak of blue fire as a kingfisher went fast downstream. She watched a handful of people waiting on the platform at Eggesford Station and the movement of sparrows quarrelling on its roof. Then, much nearer, in the rough pasture which had once been well-kept parkland, she saw something move at the base of a large chestnut tree. Its lower trunk fanned out in sloping grey buttresses and the ground around was bare and mud-trampled by the feet of sheltering cattle. Fria's eyes focussed sharply. A wood pigeon was sitting on one of the exposed roots of the tree. Fria saw its eye colour, saw each feather and the dull burnish of its breast and – though it meant nothing to her – a dried red stain on its gorget, close to the lesser coverts of its right wing. A farmer shooting the previous day had winged the pigeon and there were three or four pellets lodged in the shoulder girdle of its right wing. The bird could fly but only clumsily.

Fria recognized the bird. She knew the white patches either side of its neck and the white bars on its outer wing coverts as it flapped awkwardly from the root to the ground. She had been fed pigeons in the barn and she knew their flight from her beam-post above the loft. And she knew the succulence of their flesh. The hunger drive in her took her into the air. Maybe the ancestral memory of the peregrines' age-old craft operated independently in her. She slid away down wind in a half circle and then came back into the wind and with swift wing-beats rose and gained height. She flew fifty feet above the wood at the rear of Highford House. Down wind of her now, three hundred yards away, the pigeon moved slowly over the trampled ground close to the chestnut tree.

Fria gave three or four quick beats of her wings and went down wind fast in a long shallow stoop. A jay shrieked a warning to the world as she went over. A rabbit at the edge of the wood flattened to the ground. Fria knew nothing except the pulse of air against her as she gained speed and the figure of the pigeon growing in size as she neared it. She swept into the shadow of the tree and, although the pigeon saw her late and jumped clumsily into flight and there would have been no escape for it from an experienced peregrine, she made a complete mess of her first real attempt to take food for herself in flight. An experienced bird would have come down with its legs extended forward and tight up against its breast, the three front toes of each foot drawn up and the long rear toe daggering below, and an experienced bird would have swept close over the pigeon's back, and the deadly rear toes would have sliced into the bird. The peregrine's wings would have gone up at the moment of strike and the pigeon would have died of shock or its wound.

Fria, when she was within three yards of the pigeon, dropped her feet so that she could grab the bird with them. The movement slowed her flight and threw her off line. She grabbed at the bird as it went away below her, hit it clumsily on the left wing with a harmless, already clenched foot, and tumbled it over on its side in the air.

They came to the ground together in an untidy, flapping whirl of wings. The pigeon jumped clear and, flying low and awkwardly with its damaged right wing, headed across the pasture towards the woods. Angrily Fria went after it, flying fast and easily overtaking the injured bird. She grabbed at it again and missed as the pigeon swerved in panic and tried to gain height. But its damaged wing had no power to take it up. It skittered across the grass, hit the ground and rolled over. Fria followed and, raising her wings like a kestrel, dropped on to it.

The pigeon flapped its wings and struggled. Fria sat on it, grasping it with her strong talons, and then, instinctively to still its movements, she stabbed at the bird's neck with her beak. More by luck than design, she got a hold on the pigeon's neck and, with an angry twist of her head, broke it and the pigeon died. Fria had made her first kill.

She ate it where she had killed it, out in the open so that she would have been aware of the approach of any danger. From the pigeons she had been given in captivity she had learned how to pluck and plume them, tearing out the breast feathers. Sometimes in the past she had plucked them properly and sometimes had only made a token show before tearing at the carcase meat. Today, impatient with hunger, she plucked and ate and then plucked again as the pigeon lay on its back and she held it steady with her feet. She ate for more than half an hour. When she had finished the pigeon lay on its back in the wet grass, its wings outspread and untouched. The flesh had gone from its breast and legs. Its back was untouched, and the flesh had been cleaned from the neck. It lay there cleared down almost to the framework of the bird it had been.

Gorged, Fria rose at last from her kill and flew heavily and leisurely back to her tower and then sat in her recess and cleaned and preened herself. The experiences, clumsy and fortunate, of her first kill passed into her memory and the small store of her natural knowledge was increased.

*　*　*

Smiler was lucky. His last place of call before going home was, as usual, Highford House. This time he went to it along the road that crossed the Taw by the old stone bridge at Eggesford and

126

climbed the hill below whose crest lay Highford House. He pushed his bicycle along the lower drive that ran back from the hill road. Clear of the trees, the drive, grass-grown now, and almost vanished, crossed the pasture which had once been the park.

The light was going fast, but the patch of loose plucked feathers and the spread carcase of the pigeon stood out sharply a few yards to the right of the drive. Smiler crossed to it and knelt down. There was an immediate excitement in him. It was the first remains of a peregrine kill he had seen in the wild, but he had no difficulty in recognizing it because he had cleared such carcases away in the barn after he had fed Fria. He was delighted that Fria had to be around here somewhere and that she had – no matter how – managed to make a kill. From the way the bird had been stripped he knew that Fria must have been very hungry. In her greed she had even nipped out small pieces of the breast bone.

He gathered up the pigeon's remains and stuffed them down a rabbit hole. Left in the open, although it might have been scavenged by fox or rat, it might also be seen by a keeper. For the moment – if Fria was lodged in the vicinity – he was not keen that any keeper or farmer should find evidence of her presence.

He hurried to the old house, climbed to his vantage point and in the fading light swept his field-glasses around the close neighbourhood. He scanned the woods and the isolated tree clumps and found nothing. Most peregrines, he knew, were not keen on lodging in trees so he gave the top storeys of the old house and the red brick tower a careful survey, but he could find no sign of the falcon. Actually, he had his glasses on the ivy-screened, bramble overspill of the recess for a few seconds, but in the dim light the opening of the recess was no more than a broken patch of brickwork. Fria, bodily content, and well back in the recess, saw him as he crouched on the top parapet of the old house.

Smiler finally gave up his search as the light went. He returned to the farm, but he said nothing about finding the kill. He wanted to find Fria before he said anything to the Duchess or Bob and Bill. He could not get the next day off to search for her again. He would have to wait for the week-end. In his diary that night he confided a small doubt that had risen in his mind.

He wrote:

> . . . of course, until I've actually spotted Fria up there I can't be sure. The kill might have been made by some other peregrine. Mr. Samkin tells me that there still are a pair or two out on the cliffs near Ilfracombe. But would they have come so far inland to make a kill. Hope not. So roll on Sunday when I can have another look for her. I'd go up at night with a torch but that might be seen by people.
>
> After Mr. Samkin's tonight, that Trevor Green was waiting outside to take Sandra home. Her face! If looks could kill he'd have been a gonner.

*　　*　　*

During that week the education of Fria progressed. She caught her first field-mouse from a hovering pitch like a kestrel, her talons clamping on it through the grasses and killing it immediately. She took a starling which was running up and down the roof parapet of the old house prospecting for a nesting-site by launching herself downwards from the tower top. The starling saw her coming, panicked and, instead of diving for cover, flew upwards. Fria flicked her wings rapidly three or four times, increasing the power of her shallow stoop and then, with her momentum, threw up easily, rising almost vertically under the bird, and half-rolled and grabbed it from underneath with one foot. As she flew back to the tower she took its neck between her mandibles and broke it, the tooth in her upper mandible which fitted into a notch in the lower biting through to the vertebrae and snapping the bird's spinal cord. She was learning fast and every day discovering her latent powers. But she was still far from the perfection and smooth co-ordination of muscles, strength and deliberate intent which could take an adult peregrine at fifty or sixty miles an hour in level pursuit and at over a hundred miles an hour coming down in a vertical stoop from a height.

Fria was still hungry. Exercise and her freedom had given her an appetite bigger than she had known in captivity. Apart from the small prey, insects, mice, and the occasional small bird she might get, she needed at least the equivalent of one wood pigeon a day and, as she came back into condition, sometimes two a day. At the moment she was getting nothing like that. She was always famished and always looking for the chance to satisfy her hunger.

At first light now she was astir and spent a long time hovering over the jungled purlieus of gardens and wild shrubberies taking what she could find either from the air or by stalking on foot. As the light strengthened she would rise and fly to the woods that crested the hill and hang above them at fifty or a hundred feet watching the ground below. The birds knew her now and when she appeared over the trees they went silent and into cover.

That week she caught two more wood pigeons. The first she bungled but luck stayed with her. As she hung over the wood long after the alarm calls had died away a pigeon came flying back from the water-trough for cattle at the far end of the pasture. As it began to rise towards the first trees at the wood's edge Fria went down to cut it off. She tipped over into a slightly steeper dive, gave a flick or two of her sharp-pointed wings and angled swiftly towards the pigeon, the white flash of its wing bars showing every single covert feather in her vision, the wet gleam of its beak where it had been drinking a collection of silver reflections. Because she was above it the pigeon only saw her when she was fifty yards from it. The bird swung sideways and dipped for the cover of the shrubs at the foot of the wood's edge. Fria swung with it, curving and steepening her dive. The pigeon, knowing it would never reach cover, dropped to the ground and crashed into the base of a small gorse bush, smashing against the prickly barrier and scattering a thin shower of yellow blooms. Fria over-shot the bush. Hungry and angry, she threw up and rolled over. Seeing the dazed bird at the foot of the bush, she came down with wings raised high over her back and grabbed it with her outstretched talons. She killed it and ate it beneath the bush. It was a small bird, still with a winter thinness about it.

On the Friday she made her first clean kill. She knew now that the pigeons often used the water-trough for drinking. For two successive days she had tried for them and failed. They had seen her almost as soon as she had begun her dive and had wheeled away and found the sanctuary of the wood in good time.

Whether Fria reasoned out the cause of her failure or whether chance showed her the solution could be long debated without resolution for only she could know. But on the Friday a warm air current rose strongly from the wood below, smooth and without turbulence. She found herself circling easily at a much higher pitch, well over two hundred feet. When she saw a pigeon coming back from the trough she angled over and went into her dive with fast wing strokes. Her height and the position of the pigeon made her attack take a much steeper line. She found herself going down in a half-vertical stoop, faster than ever she had gone, except for a few times when the gale had whipped her away from the barn. And as she went she automatically, instinctively now, put her legs forward and close up to her breast, talons tightly clenched, to keep the air stream slipping smoothly past her body. With her wings almost closed she streaked downwards and the pigeon left this life without seeing her. As she hurled past it she dropped her legs to make a grabbing movement at the bird, but her speed was so fast that she hit it with clenched talons on the side of the neck. A puff of feathers exploded from the blow, and the pigeon, dead with a broken neck and shock, rolled over and tumbled to the ground in an untidy swirl of limp wings and legs and a following gentle parachuting of small feathers.

Fria opened her wings, braked against the speed of her dive and, without gaining height, slewed round in a fast circle, low over the pasture, and came back to the pigeon. She settled on it, grasped it with her talons and flew low and clumsily with it in the direction of her tower. But the bird was heavy and as she reached Highford House she dropped down with it and settled on one of the broad parapet ledges where she ate it.

Late that afternoon she took a lapwing which was grub-hunting in the parkland grass. She did it from the same high pitch which gave her the element of surprise, but the kill was not made with the ripping blow of her rear toes as an experienced falcon would have made it. She hit it with clenched talons dropped. The blow killed the rising bird with its stunning force and she went down after it. This time she carried the lapwing easily to her tower and ate it on the roof above her recess.

7

∾ Strangers in the Mist ∾

On Sunday morning as soon as he had finished breakfast Smiler hurried off to Highford House. Since it was only a couple of miles from the farm, he went on foot and across country to it.

He reached the house just after nine o'clock and climbed to his favourite parapet lookout. He was determined to sit there all day and, if Fria was around, to find her. In the pocket of his storm-coat were a packet of sandwiches and a can of cider which the Duchess had given him.

It was a warm morning without wind, balmy, with a strong touch of Spring mildness. The sky was cloudless. Blue and long-tailed tits belled in the shrubberies and worked the slowly budding branches of trees and bushes for food. The wood was full of birdsong and far below him the river meadows were free of flood water. The river itself was beginning to clear in colour and the salmon and sea-trout were running. Through his glasses as he swept them round searching for Fria, Smiler saw two fish jump in the pool below Eggesford bridge. But he saw no sign of Fria. Half an hour before he had arrived Fria had killed one of a flock of black-headed gulls that had come inland, following the river. They had been foraging in the pasture of the old parkland. She had flown at them from her tower, dropping low and going very fast, not more than two feet above the ground, towards the flock. They had gone up as she was almost on them in a cloud of white and grey wings. She had swung upwards under one of them, rolled on to her back and grabbed at the bird's breast and made the easiest kill she had ever known. She had carried the bird to the edge of the wood and eaten it, and then, full and contented, had flown up to the lower limb of an ancient oak, made her toilet, and now sat there in the sun. She was hidden from Smiler by a yew tree standing next to the oak, its glossy evergreen foliage screening the lower part of the oak tree.

After an hour's watching Smiler got restless and walked and scrambled around the parapet of the house. He found the carcase of the pigeon which Fria had eaten there and this gave him fresh hope. He found another viewpoint from a different part of the roof and sat down with his back against a stone slab, enjoying the sunshine. He had been working hard all week and was now doing an extra night's session with Mr. Samkin, and he had worked all day Saturday. Within half an hour he was asleep.

Ten minutes later Fria came flying back to her tower recess. She saw Smiler sleeping on the roof, swerved a little from her line, and landed on the tower. She dropped down to the recess, shuffled in, gave a little shake to settle her breast feathers and folded her long wings over her tail. She was well fed for the moment and she dozed.

Half an hour later Smiler woke up. He rolled over on the long parapet ledge and, resting his chin on his hands, stared idly through the small gap in the roof ledge which had been cut for the rain water to run off into a now non-existent gutter. He had a funnelled view of the woods and shrubberies that crowded close to the old garden.

A movement in the rhododendron bushes caught his eye, a quick, pinky-white flicker. He reached for his glasses and focussed on the spot. Clear in the lens was the face of Jimmy Jago. He was standing in the cover of the shrubs watching the tower and house.

Smiler was puzzled. For a moment his delight in seeing Jimmy almost made him move to stand up and wave to him. Then he remembered the other times when he had seen Jimmy here at night. He stayed still, watching. Something was wrong between Jimmy and the Duchess. He was sure, if their quarrel had been patched up, she would have told him and certainly have said if Jimmy were coming back to the farm. Smiler decided that it was wiser to stay hidden where he was. "Whatever's going on between those two, Samuel M.," he told himself, "it's private to them or they would have told you."

Jimmy kept his station at the fringe of the shrubbery for five minutes and then moved, taking advantage of every piece of cover, crouching now and then to keep his figure clear of any sky-line. He passed between the tower and the back of the house, and Smiler held him in his glasses. He seemed so near that Smiler felt he could put out a hand and touch him. He wore a battered felt hat, a shabby, green windbreaker and crumpled, brown corduroy trousers. But the thing that interested Smiler most was that in one hand he carried a small white envelope. Smiler could see it plainly.

As Jimmy passed out of his line of sight around the far corner of the house Smiler wondered what on earth he could be doing up here with a letter and – without doubt – not at all anxious to be seen by anyone.

Smiler stayed where he was, unmoving, but keeping his glasses trained on the place where Jimmy had gone out of his sight. After a few minutes Jimmy reappeared and went quickly and unobtrusively back to the woods beyond the tower. Smiler saw at once that he no longer carried the white envelope with him.

Puzzled and intrigued, Smiler watched Jimmy disappear. He sat there for fifteen minutes to make sure that Jimmy had really gone. His curiosity growing stronger each moment, he decided that it could not do any harm to go down and see if he could find out where Jimmy had put the letter. The whole thing was a mystery and – although it was none of his business – his curiosity was too strong to be denied. He was not going to take the letter if he found it. He just wanted to know what was going on – and then, since it involved Jimmy, keep his mouth shut.

Sure that Jimmy had now gone, he was on the point of rising when the whole affair was driven completely from his mind. Fria launched herself from her recess, dropped low over the garden for a moment, then rose and half-keeled over so that she swept the length of the house parapet, passing within two feet of Smiler. He watched transfixed. She was so close that he could see the nostril holes of her strong hooked beak and the brightness of her dark eyes framed in her brown-black mask lines. Her wings and back seemed a darker slate colour than he remembered. She held her legs up loosely towards her breast and the brightening yellow of their skin gleamed in the sun as from her half-canted position she suddenly rolled right over in flight and moved away.

"*Blimey Old Riley*," Smiler breathed to himself, "*she's super!*" His excitement was suddenly so strong that it sent a shiver through him and made the skin of his cheek-bones tingle and would have brought tears to his eyes if he had not sniffed hard. He raised his glasses and found her in them, watching every movement. There was no other thought in his head but of Fria.

Fria, having eaten well and had her doze, had moved from her recess in order to satisfy another want. Since she had left the barn beam the only bath she had taken was in a largish puddle that had formed on the tower leads after the heavy rain. But the feel of the lead beneath her feet was like the slippery tin of the old bath she had used in captivity and the puddle was only half an inch deep. Knowing what she wanted, knowing where she could find it, Fria was in no hurry.

Now that Smiler had found her – though he had not seen her come out of the recess on the tower – it was almost as though she wanted to go through her paces for him, to show him that she was well on the way to being able to look after herself and that her dawning new powers were giving her a confidence in herself which was half the battle of survival.

In actual fact Fria had no thought for Smiler at all. She had seen and marked him as she went by the roof, but as she beat up and over the far pasture woods she was obsessed with a spirit of playfulness which she had never known before.

Watched by Smiler, she ringed up leisurely over the woods, circling on an air current, and only now and then giving a quick flick of her wings to speed her climb. She went up five hundred feet and then hung at her station in a slow level swing that was a couple of hundred yards in diameter. She went idly round and round and every bird in the wood and beyond it was aware of her. But by some magic of communication they knew that she was no threat, or maybe it was that there was a subtle difference in the style of her flight that told them she hung high, not in menace, but in the enjoyment of the slow ecstasy of her own powers.

From her curving pitch Fria marked a solitary crow perched at the top of the chestnut tree in the old parkland. She rolled over, half closed her wings, and went down in a fast dive which was the extent of her stooping powers so far. Five seconds later she whipped over the top of the crow, two feet above him, and threw up. For the first time ever she went up vertically and let herself go until all the momentum had gone from her body. She levelled out and hovered, looking down at the crow who, in the moment of her pass at him, had thrown himself backwards, raising black beak to ward off danger and had then fallen clumsily into a tangle of twigs and branches where he was now croaking curses at her.

Glasses on her, Smiler laughed and fidgeted with delight, and for the next five minutes the world was forgotten as he watched Fria's first display of play, the need for which is instinctive in all peregrines.

She went fast along the edge of the wood, six feet from the ground and chased a green woodpecker which was coming in from the pasture in a lazy looping flight. Fria went up under the bird, rolled on her back, just brushed him with her talons clenched, and was gone; beating high on quick wings before the bird knew what had happened. On pitch again, and a little higher this time, she came down over the green length of a fir plantation and chased a passing wood pigeon, whose eyes – from experience – were all for danger from the ground below, not the sky above. She passed inches above him. The bird slewed downwards in a plummeting panic dive for the cover of the pines. She swung upwards in a tight circle, going over on her back, and came out at the bottom of the circle and overtook the pigeon six feet above the nearest pine-tip, flashing by him in play, crying to herself and exhilarated by the tight vertical loop she had made for the first time in her life.

Then, pressed by her real need, she came back fast towards Smiler. She passed with a hiss of wings between the tower and the old house and slanted down the valley-side to the river. Some way below Eggesford bridge the valley woods reached right down to the river and the overhanging trees on either bank made a tunnel through which the Taw raced over a rocky bed. She dipped low over the river and went fast down the tunnel.

The white flick of a dipper on a moss-topped rock in mid-stream caught her eye. Fria swerved and came down almost to water level and dropped one leg to pick the bird off as she passed. But the dipper, which had survived many a sparrowhawk's similar corsair attack, dived under the water, running along the stony bed for a couple of yards before surfacing and flying into the cover of some dead nettles on the bank.

A few hundred yards down the river Fria found a pool left in a rock basin by the dropping river and she settled and took her bath.

On the roof of Highford House Smiler sat in a quiet trance. The last he had seen of Fria had been her plunge into the river tunnel. The glasses idle in his hands on his lap, he just sat and shook his head in wonderment. The ruffled, spiritless bird of the barn was gone. He knew that this was the beginning of a new Fria, and from what he had seen of her display he guessed that she had now found she was able to take food for herself. He had no more worry about that.

An hour later Fria came back. She had bathed and then made her toilet on the branch of an oak hanging over the river.

Smiler saw her coming up the valley side and

put his glasses on her. In the talons of her right leg, dangling a little below her body, she held the body of a dipper which had not been so fortunate as the first one. She flew to the tower-top and settled. Holding the dipper with one claw, she began to plume and eat it. When she had finished she cleaned her beak, preened her breast feathers and then dropped down and settled on the ledge of the recess. For a moment she raised her wings, half-arching them above her back, flexing the muscles, and then shuffled into her quarters.

With the last of the light going from the sky Smiler made his way back to the farm, the joy and excitement which were still in him making him kick out at odd stones on his path and swing with a hazel stick he had picked up at the dead heads of last year's foxgloves and tansies.

*   *   *

Back at the farm while he was having supper Smiler suddenly remembered Jimmy Jago.

He said to the Duchess, "Have you heard at all from Mr. Jimmy, ma'am?"

"Not for two weeks. He was in Newcastle then. Did you have any luck with Fria?"

Smiler realized that she had changed the subject deliberately and he knew enough about grown-ups now to ask no more questions. He had his own evasions to practise, too. Fria was his, and the last thing he wanted was a lot of people knowing where she was. At some time or other he knew that someone must see her flying, but it was ten to one that they would think she was a falcon that had come inland from the far coast and would not be tempted to go searching for her. Since he had no good reason to ask the Duchess to keep the discovery a secret (and knowing, too, that she had many friends with whom she loved to gossip) he said diplomatically, "She's around Eggesford way by the look of it. I found a pigeon she'd killed and eaten."

The Duchess smiled to herself. Though he had tried to cover it, she had noticed the excitement in Smiler when he had returned. In her own mind she was sure he had found Fria. Being an understanding woman, she had decided that if he did not want to be frank with her it must be for some good reason of his own.

For the rest of that week Smiler only managed to get very short glimpses of Fria. He had found that by eating his lunch quickly he had just time enough to run up to Highford House and spend a few minutes there before he had to get back to his afternoon work. If he missed this expedition there was just enough light now as the evenings lengthened with March's going to give him a short time up at the house before night fell. Mostly Fria was sitting on the tower-top or the recess ledge when he arrived, since she liked to hunt in the morning or late afternoon.

The following week-end he spent most of his time up there. While Fria was away from the tower he went inside and climbed the stairs as high as he dared go. There was a twenty-foot gap before the remains of the top flight began again. The narrow lancet windows of the tower were either boarded over or smothered in ivy growths so that it was dark inside. The darkness gave away the position of Fria's ledge, for the daylight angled into the tower through the small gap in the bricks at its rear. As Smiler stared up at the shaft of light it suddenly flickered and then was blotted out. He ran outside and, with his glasses, saw from his parapet that Fria had returned and gone into the recess.

That Fria was getting enough food now he had no doubt. Often, as he explored through the woods around the hill, he came on the remains of her kills and could easily identify them. There were more wood pigeons than anything else, but Smiler also came across black-headed gulls, lapwings and partridges – and once, where the railway passed over the river above Eggesford, the remains of a tufted duck lying on the gangers' track at the side of the line.

Since he could not always be borrowing Mr. Samkin's binoculars, Smiler took all his savings from his wages and the little money he had brought to Devon with him and bought himself a pair of second-hand glasses in Barnstaple one week-end. They were not as good as Mr. Samkin's but they were good enough to satisfy Smiler.

Mr. Samkin said to him one night after Sandra had left, "You never want my field-glasses now."

Rather wooden-faced, Smiler said, "No, sir. Thank you." For some reason which he found it hard to explain to himself he did not want to say a word about his discovery of Fria and her progress in adapting herself to her new life.

Mr. Samkin gave a little smile. He could read Smiler like a book and he could have explained to him his reasons for wanting to say nothing about Fria.

He said, "I'm not going to put you in the witness-box, Samuel, and grill you. Field-glasses are as personal a possession to a sensitive man as his watch, his fountain pen, or his trout or salmon rod . . . even if he has to fit himself out with second-hand ones to begin with. And don't worry too much about people around here. Most of them never lift their eyes above the horizontal. They only know the sun is shining because they feel the heat on the top of their heads. But there are some whose eyes miss nothing. Nine out of ten of them give thanks for what they may see and keep their own counsel. The tenth is a scoundrel, and damned be his name, for profit is his god."

Before he could stop himself, Smiler blurted out, "I know where she is, sir. But I don't want to say, even to you, please, sir."

Mr. Samkin, with a twinkle in his eyes, said, "You don't have to tell me anything, Samuel. I go for long walks. I have eyes in my head."

April came and, as was the custom each year, Bob and Bill brought out the painted tent from the barn store and set it up on the small lawn. On fine afternoons the Duchess would sit in its doorway, with Scampi in attendance, and knit or just enjoy the sun and her own thoughts. Now and again someone would come for a consultation and the Duchess would oblige them.

The hawthorns were in half leaf and the ashes

began to show green. Spring was stirring and the early blackbirds and thrushes had already laid their eggs, though not so soon as the sparrows and the starlings which haunted the barns and the farm buildings.

Fria was used to hunting for herself now, though she was still far from possessing all the skills of an experienced peregrine. Her condition had improved; the yellow skin of her legs was now almost buttercup-coloured and the slack, half-hardened quills of her primary, secondary and tail feathers had firmed up. She flew with a compact, powerful rhythm. She fed well, sometimes taking two wood pigeons or their equivalent each day. But she never killed without hunger. She killed only to eat, and death came swiftly as her hooked beak bit into a bird's neck, jerked, and snapped through the neck column.

But, now, for some reason beyond her understanding, she found herself impelled to strange moods, mostly at first light. She would fly to the tower-top or sometimes to the tall crest of a near-by oak and sit wailing softly to herself or shuffling to and fro, croaking and talking to herself, and then suddenly raise her wings and beat them in quick spasms without taking to the air. Only after she had killed did the mood leave her.

*   *   *

In the first week in April Johnny Pickering got another letter. It read: LEAVE IT TOO LATE AND YOU KNOW YOUR FATE.

Worse still, as he went out of his house to go to work, he found a police patrol car parked on the opposite side of the road. As he bicycled away the car started and slowly began to follow him. Before he could help himself he began to ride quickly, touched with panic, and his heart almost stopped as the car passed him. He waited to see whether it would draw in ahead. But the car went on and swung down a side turning. The two policemen in the car were completely uninterested in him. They had merely stopped in the road to send a message over the radio on a matter which in no way concerned Johnny Pickering. But Johnny Pickering had had a nasty moment and was far from recovered from it when he reached work.

In that first week of April Smiler had a letter, too. It was one which sent him out to his morning work whistling his head off. Laura had written to say that there was a good chance that at the end of April or the begining of May – by dint of much badgering of her parents – she would be coming down for a short holiday to Devon and could Smiler find her rooms or a lodging somewhere near him? "But I can't give you the proper dates yet because it depends how the work goes here on the farm. And my father's not whole-hearted convinced about me going yet (though he will be) because to hear him carry on you'd think I was a bairn in arms still and Devon as far away as Australia. Parents! (Though Mother's all on my side I fancy.) The latest from himself is that – if he lets me go – I'll have to pay my own railway fare, but he'll have to reckon with Mother over that."

So Smiler went whistling about his work as though, Bob said, he had swallowed a canary.

And on the Friday morning of that first week in April, the mist for which Maxie had been praying for weeks and weeks without the weather obliging, came to the moor.

*　　*　　*

It came down at three o'clock in the afternoon. The sky was overcast with low, barely moving clouds, and there was the faintest fret of a drizzle in the air. Slowly the distant tors and stretches of the moor were lost in what seemed a thickening of the air. Then, suddenly, the drizzle fined and became a veiling of mist which changed rapidly into a grey-white blanket that cut all visibility down to a hundred yards and still closed in.

In the quarry where Maxie was working, watched by the warder guards, a whistle blew and was followed by shouts from the warders for the prisoners to cease work and to assemble on the quarry bed to be marshalled for the march back to Princetown Gaol.

Maxie dropped the sledge hammer with which he had been breaking up stones and began to walk towards the assembly point. As he went, the mist thickened and the warders' calls became harsh and demanding. Maxie knew that his moment was coming. He walked slowly, judging the quick thickening of the mist and the dwindling distance between himself and the men and warders beginning to congregate in the quarry.

He was fifteen yards from the group when a heavy pall of mist swirled slowly across the quarry and the group was lost for a moment. Maxie dropped to his knees behind a quarried block of stone, rolled over, and let himself fall off the small track into a cushion of heather and tall grasses below a small bank. He rose and stooping low began to run away from the group, following a small water gully that sloped upwards to the low crest of the quarry.

Maxie was a strong, fit man and he had not allowed prison life to soften him. He went as fast as he could now, knowing that every yard he made before his absence was discovered would be precious, and he knew exactly which course to take. For months he had studied the quarry area and the wide sweeps of the moors around it. The knowledge was a vivid map in his mind which he followed unerringly. He had the true countryman's gift of a feeling for his surroundings, of carrying in his mind small and large patterns of the twists and turns of streams and tracks, and of sensing his direction from the drift of the mist and the wind-angled lean of bushes and isolated trees.

Behind him, suddenly, there was the shout of alarmed voices and then the blowing of whistles. He knew exactly what had happened. He had been missed. As he ran he could picture the scene. The men would be marshalled in a tight file, a couple of warders would be checking the roll-call again while another warder would already be on his radio link alerting the prison authorities in Princetown. He knew, too, that in this mist none

148

of the warders would come after him. They had the other prisoners to keep safe and they knew that if the mist for the moment was Maxie's friend it could also in a few hours become his enemy. To make a breakaway was one thing – and many men had tried it – but to keep going through the mist, knowingly and unerringly following a line to safety, was a task few men could accomplish successfully. Within half an hour there would be blocks formed on all the moor roads. The moment the mist lifted, search parties would begin to comb the moor, and with daylight there would be a helicopter or two to help them.

But for the moment Maxie was safe and he was away. Within half an hour, too, rumour would run through the prison itself.

"There's one away."

"Who?"

"Maxie Martin – the Gypo."

"Good luck to 'im."

Five minutes later, swinging slowly round in a circle to bring him on a north- instead of the south-bearing line of his escape, Maxie crossed the main Princetown–Tavistock road. He jumped the far ditch, found the remembered stone wall of a small field and headed along it. At the top of the field he climbed the upper wall and dropped down to the heather and short sheep-bitten turf of the moor.

At the meeting-point of the field's side and top stone walls, he took his line from their right angle. Loping at an easy pace he began to head steadily through the mist, the daylight fading, and prayed, but without any panic, that within the next half-mile he would hit the broad mark which would be his true route to that night's sanctuary. After a while, although he was going steadily uphill, the ground began to fall away to his right, plugs of grey stone breaking its face and then, muted but unmistakable through the mist, came the sound of running water.

He went caterways down the slope and found his mark, a small stream, cascading and rippling down the bottom of a boggy-floored combe. Maxie, keeping just clear of the miry ground, began to work his way up the stream. His confidence rose for it was far from the first time in his life that he had used this route. There had been a time when he and Jimmy Jago, blood brothers, had caught the small, hungry trout in the stream, had poached the odd lamb from the moor flocks and – but less often – had cut out some foal from the herds of moor ponies to take away to be sold or used for caravan work eventually. He smiled to himself as he remembered the odd times when some snorting, angry moor stallion had come charging at them to protect its progeny – though at the time it had been no laughing matter. And it was no laughing matter now. He was away and he was going to stay away. Princetown was never going to see him again. . . . He'd sooner die first, for wasn't that better for a real man than being shut up like a rat in a cage for years and years and the heart's truth sounding clear as a bell that the law was one thing, but justice another?

After an hour of slow progress the ground grew

marshier. He had to stop now and then to pick up the sound of the water to his right. He came out finally on to a wide, sedgy, peat-bogged plateau from which the stream rose. He circled the bog to the west and picked up through the mist a broken stone wall, studded here and there with a twisted thorn. In its lee was a narrow track. He followed this, scaring small parties of sheep that now and then loomed out of the mist, hearing the thud of their feet as they went away into the gloom, until the wall ended. Then he swung left-handed, well above the stream's boggy source.

He began to climb now, edging his way up the long easy slope of a moorland tor. But he had to go slowly for the darkness had come and, although his eyes had made some adjustment to the misty gloom, he knew that one rash step, a trip over a rock outcrop, could twist an ankle or break a leg and take all chance of freedom from him. He reached the top of the tor after an hour, recognizing it, knowing where he was from times past. There was a small ring of stones enclosing a bare arena from which he heard the sound of sheep scattering as he entered it. He sat down with his back against a rock and rested. From a small flat tin which every day for months he had fixed with adhesive tape under his left armpit and worn whenever he went out on a working party, he took a small section of chocolate and ate it slowly. Then he took one of the five cigarettes the tin held and lit it with one of the red-tipped matches in the tin, striking the match against the face of the rock. He smoked contentedly, knowing himself safe from pursuit while the mist lasted, knowing, too, that he was safely on his proper route. Another two hours would take him to the cache at the bottom of Hangingstone Hill where Jimmy Jago had promised to leave provisions and a change of clothes for him.

As he sat there he sensed that the mist was beginning to thin a little and there was the faintest suggestion of a breeze stirring. That did not surprise him. It was April and late for any heavy, prolonged mist. But the mist had given him all he needed now. Once he reached the cache and could get rid of his prison clothes he knew that he could make the rest of his journey, the first stage to freedom. He sat there, high above the moor, alone, and content with his isolation.

But Maxie Martin was not alone. Fifty feet from him, across the other side of the small circle, sat another stranger in the mist whose ears had heard his approach; whose eyes had caught the small flare of the match: who sat, now, perched twelve feet up on a granite outcrop and, as the wind thinned or parted the slow veils of mist, could see the shadowed figure of Maxie sitting with his back to his rock.

It was a peregrine tiercel, a full adult in its third season. It sat there, humped against the mist and darkness, looking like a spur of the rock on which it sat.

It was a tiercel born in a Welsh eyrie. Its falcon and tiercel parents had been one of a few pairs of Welsh peregrines which, out of lingering atavistic compulsion, made the passage from their birthplace far south to the high passes and lonely peaks of the Spanish Pyrenees to winter. Adult now, the tiercel had long lost all contact with its parents. The previous year it had mated and, out of a clutch of four eggs, only one had hatched to give the world an eyas falcon which had been shot by a Welsh chicken farmer long before the time had come for it to make its passage to Spain. The brood falcon had started her passage four days before the tiercel and had been trapped in the chestnut woods above Canterets by flying into a fine nylon net hung between two trees as she dived after a pigeon. She had been sold to a Spanish falconer.

The tiercel that sat on the rock close to Maxie now was in passage back to his Welsh hills. He had rested the previous night on the cliffs of Belle Ile off Quiberon in the Bay of Biscay. In the morning he had beat up three thousand feet and, aided by a mild southerly wind, had crossed the Brittany peninsular, meeting the coast at St. Brieuc. He had winged his way north without urgency over the Channel Islands and hit the English coast at Start Point in Devon. On the southern slopes of Dartmoor he had dropped to a small river and had drunk and bathed and rested.

Late in the afternoon he had taken off and, hungry, had moved up the moor, two thousand feet high, his eyes watching the vast spread of ground below him. The migrant birds were arriving. He marked the small movement of whinchat, stonechat and warblers and, once, the hawk shape of a cuckoo quick-flighting along a shallow moorland combe. Far below the skylarks hovered and sang and he saw a covey of partridges break cover near the Princetown–Tavistock road. The tiercel watched the movement of cars along the road, saw clearly the shine on the swinging points of pickaxes being used in the small quarry by the prisoners, and the network of small streams, gathering to become rivers, that flowered from the high reaches of the moor. Over a moorland farm, the lichens and moss on its slate roof clear to him, he saw the flight movement of three pigeons, flying high and in formation. They were a kit of three flying tipplers – a breed of domestic pigeons trained, not as homers for long-distance flying, but for endurance in the air. Flown in competition by their trainers they could circuit, sometimes as high as two thousand feet, for as long as twenty hours in the air before being called or forced down from exhaustion.

The tipplers were fifteen hundred feet below the tiercel and flying in an inverted V formation. The tiercel winged over, dropped his head and stooped, picking up speed with a few rapid, sharp-cutting beats of his wings. He came down the sky almost vertically, wings closed, legs thrust forward and close up to his breast, talons clenched, his speed increasing with each second. He struck the leading tippler at eighty miles an hour, dropping his right leg and ripping into the base of the bird's neck with an extended rear talon. As the pigeon's feathers exploded about him, the tiercel threw up into a tight vertical circle as the two other pigeons dropped, zig-zagging and panic-flighting, for the farmhouse roof a half a mile away. The tiercel, wind singing against his half-opened wings, went down after the tumbling, dead bird. He grasped it out of the air a hundred feet above ground and flew heavily with it on a long slant that took him to the top of the tor where he now was perched.

There he had eaten it, preened himself, rested a while, and then the mist had come down cloaking him suddenly with dampness and gloom. The tiercel hated flying in thick rain, thunder clouds, or in mist. He stayed where he was, restless at first, making small cries now and then to himself, and later quietening as the night slowly joined the mist and darkness closed in.

He sat now watching the red glow of Maxie's cigarette-end pulse and wane as the man smoked. Only the thick mist, which would cloak and confuse him if he took to flight, kept the tiercel there.

Two hours later the tiercel still sat on the granite rock spur. The mist was thinning slowly. He would sit now until first light. Five miles away Maxie had found the cache and the trowel which Jimmy Jago had hidden. He sat on the ground and dug the waterproofed haversack free. Inside were clothes, a pack of food, a small flask of brandy, a pencil-slim torch, cigarettes and a lighter, and an envelope with ten one-pound notes in it. These notes he knew were only a reserve in case he was forced to abandon his journey towards the sanctuary which had been prepared for him at Highford House.

He stripped himself completely of all his prison

clothes and of his socks and boots. When he was dressed in the outfit which Jimmy had provided, he buried all his old clothing in the cache hole and covered it with earth.

The mist was thin now and the wind had freshened. Maxie occasionally caught glimpses of the sky and the stars above him. He dropped down the torside and flanked the edges of the mire which was part of the spongy womb from which the stripling Taw found life. When he reached the little combe through which the Taw first began to run with any strength and definition he stopped. Flask in hand he knelt beside it, leaned over and sucked at the water to drink. Then he took a swig from the brandy flask. Before he stood up he reached his hand into the water and splashed it over his face and the back of his neck, talking to himself in the language which the Duchess and Jimmy used between them. The libation was not done for the sake of coolness. It was a ritual thanksgiving born of sentiment and an acknowledgment of the magic which from the dawn of time all water had carried for primitive man and his descendants. And for this particular water Maxie had a special reverence for he had been born within sight and sound of it in a caravan in a field on the river bank below the village of Brushford Barton.

Just before first light Maxie left the growing river and made a detour around the village of Sticklepath which lay on the main road between Okehampton and Exeter, a road which was the northern boundary of the moor, every yard of which in daylight would hold danger for him. He crossed it with the last of the mist and rejoined the river a mile farther north.

And, with the first light, back on the moor the tiercel shook his body and head, splaying and shuffling his feathers free of mist drops and the discomfort of the night. He dropped from his rock, flew across the small tor-top arena and then rose leisurely into the air, climbing up on the breast of a mild northerly wind, leaving behind him the early soaring and singing larks, moving up and up until he should be satisfied with a pitch from which he could, a speck in the sky lost to the world below, move on towards the eyrie of his birth.

8

✑ *Spring Courtship* ✑

That morning – which was a Saturday – Smiler told the Duchess over breakfast about Laura's letter and asked her if she knew anyone in the district who would be able to give her lodgings.

"She's coming sometime at the end of the month, or the beginning of May, ma'am."

The Duchess eyed him quizzically across the table and said, "With her parents' approval, I hope?"

"Oh, yes, of course. Her father's being a bit difficult right now, but Laura and her mother will see to him."

The Duchess chuckled. "I don't doubt it. What chance would one man have against two females? Well now, let's see. Lodgings. Mr. Samkin has a room that he lets sometimes if specially asked."

"Oh, I wouldn't want Laura to be up there. I mean, Mr. Samkin's nice and all that . . . but well, he teaches me and it could be a bit difficult of an evening if I was up there studying. . . ."

The Duchess chuckled. "You mean your mind wouldn't be on your work with Laura in the house? Well, then, what about the Parsons? They take in visitors during the summer. They'd have a room. And Sandra would be company for her while you're working – unless you were thinking of asking for the week off?"

"I hadn't exactly thought of that, ma'am. But I don't fancy Sandra and Laura together."

The Duchess laughed. "No – and I don't fancy that they would fancy it."

Smiler said after a moment's pause, "I was wondering . . ."

"Yes?"

Embarrassed, Smiler said quickly, "No, I couldn't."

"You couldn't what?"

Smiler shook his head. "No, it doesn't matter. I'll ask Bob and Bill. They'll know some place."

"You won't ask them anything, Sammy. And I can't think why you're making such a bowl of porridge about the whole thing. You know perfectly well what you've got in mind. There's another spare room here. You'd like her to stay here, wouldn't you?"

"Oh, ma'am – could she? She could help about the house and farm and she's a good cook——"

"And what sort of holiday would that be? No, the matter's settled. She can stay here and she doesn't have to pay a penny or do a hand's turn unless the fancy takes her. Maybe, too, we might arrange it that you have a week's holiday while she's here. But not if I don't get an extra special good report on your work from Mr. Samkin. He's not particularly pleased with your Latin at the moment."

"I know. I don't seem to get on with it very well."

"Well, you'd better get on with it if you want a week's holiday. But no matter what – Laura stays here."

"That's super, ma'am. You're very good to me, ma'am."

The Duchess grinned. "Now you're buttering me up. But don't think because I've got a soft spot for you that I'll give you a week's holiday just at a flicker of those blue eyes of yours. Latin will get you that."

Smiler went out to work whistling. From the kitchen where she was washing up the Duchess heard him. With a shake of her head at Scampi, sunning himself on the windowsill, and a grin, she said, "Men."

She reached out and turned on the radio for the regional news. The first item she heard was an account of the escape of a Princetown prisoner, Maxie Martin. Her face showed no surprise. The weather report the previous night had mentioned the mist over Dartmoor. The two went together and, for weeks now, she had known that one day they would. Her mind went back, as it had often done, to the morning she had taken Smiler into the painted tent and the crystal ball had shown her the figure of a blood-spattered running man and would have shown her more had she not closed her eyes against it. She switched off the radio.

As she did so, some twenty miles to the south of Bullaybrook Farm Maxie had gone to ground for the day. Following the river in daylight was a risk he would not take, a risk he did not have to take because the one commodity he possessed in abundance was time. He had climbed the slope of a rough pasture on the river-bank into a broad stand of dark firs. Some way in the wood was a small clearing where trees had been felled. One quick look around showed him that nobody had been working in the clearing for days. At the side of the clearing was a large pile of green-needled branches and slim fir tops that had been trimmed off the felled trees. Maxie burrowed into the pile, made himself a rough but not uncomfortable couch and then pulled loose branches over the opening, forming a screen thick enough to hide him but through which he could watch the clearing. He opened a tin of sardines and ate them with some biscuits from his store. Then he lay watching the clearing as the daylight strengthened. Around him the birds' dawn chorus gathered strength. For the first time that year he heard the chiff-chaff, the tolling of a cuckoo, and the lyrical, rippling notes of a willow warbler with its dying fall down the scale. A dog fox came to the edge of the clearing, sunlight gleaming briefly on its chestnut flanks, scented him and turned back into the firs. Maxie lay there content with his freedom, confident in his own skills and the loyalty of friends to preserve it for him.

*   *   *

The tiercel was in no hurry. He soared above the lightening land at three thousand feet and then, finding an air current, went lazily up on it into the fire-streaked glory of a cloudless, dawn sky. He went so high that no human eye from below could have followed him and then he side-slipped free of the rising column of air and winged northwards slowly.

The whole horizon was his except for the narrow wedge of view that flared away behind him in a broadening segment from his tail. He rocked now and then and below him the land tipped and swung like a coloured compass-card on its gimbals. He saw the white foam of water over the weirs of the Taw miles away, the smoke and dawn haze over distant Barnstaple and Bideford, and the pewter spread of the estuary and sea slowly being burnished by the rising sun. He loitered, idle and wandering, sometimes swinging out to the west and then curving in a great circle following the invisible coil of an air current that up-cushioned his almost fixed wings. The sun rose clear of the eastern reaches of the land and burned in an orange-red ball through the faint morning haze. The sky brightened, waking the pink and cream colours of farmhouse and cottage walls, silvering the slates of narrow church steeples and burdening the movement of bullock, cows and sheep at graze with long black shadows.

A thousand feet below, a flock of sandpipers flew northwards, making the quick passage from the South Devon coast to the Bristol Channel and beyond in their migratory flight back from Africa. Their sharp, musical trilling voices came up to him clearly as they chattered on the wing. He watched the quick flick of their white-barred wings, the play of light over their bronze backs and, on a sudden impulse, he tipped over and went down after them. He gave eight quick wing strokes in two seconds to speed his stoop, closed his wings, the long primaries folding slightly over his tail, and dropped like a dark spearhead. Within seconds he was stooping at well over eighty miles an hour and the ravished air hissed away from his body with a thin, tearing sound. But there was no hunger in him.

He marked the leading bird and shot past it a couple of inches from its tail. As the flock scattered in confusion, their panic cries filling the air, the tiercel threw up fifty feet below them and soared upwards, bursting through their ragged ranks. Then he rolled over, rocked on his wings, and watched them streaming earthwards, seeking the cover of the woods and river-bank below. He called *krek-krek-krek* after them and then drifted away to the north, watching the line of the river below and the worming movement of a train coming along the tracks between main road and river.

A little later he was over the church at Eggesford above the left bank of the Taw. Then, directly below him were the ruined house and tower of Highford. Over a thousand feet below he saw the figure of Fria sitting on the tower-top. He recognized at once the larger shape and size of a falcon. He flew on, and had the sharp-curving wriggle of the Bullay brook below him. He marked Smiler driving a tractor loaded with hurdles across one of the brook fields, saw Bob leading one of the horses across the yard, and the Duchess's white line of washing fluttering in the strengthening morning breeze.

Suddenly he turned, edged round in a half-circle and with quick wing-beats flew back along his course until he was over Highford House again. He circled at a thousand feet, watching Fria below, and wailed gently.

Fria made no movement. But she had seen the tiercel. She had seen him the first time he had flown over, and she watched him now. He swung round in a great circle and then came back, sliding lower down the sky and calling again. Watching him, Fria shuffled her feet a little and bobbed her head out of the excitement suddenly in her of seeing one of her own kind. The tiercel dropped lower in a short stoop, rolled twice in display and, flattening out, swung round the large chestnut in the old parkland. He came back to the ruined house and passed a hundred feet over Fria with a slow rocking movement of his wings.

The tiercel flew over her three times, wailing gently now and again. Fria followed his movements bobbing her head and shuffling her feet.

The tiercel came back and settled on the roof parapet of the old house. He sat there, shook his feathers into place, and stared fiercely across at Fria. Both birds sat for five minutes without stirring and then, suddenly, the tiercel flew across to the tower and settled on the far side of the leads from Fria. She turned and faced him across the tower top.

The tiercel, like all males, was only about a third of the size of the falcon. His back was a darker slate-colour than Fria's, and his breast, grey-barred, was creamier. But though smaller there was a strength and compactness about his bearing which Fria still lacked. His feet were as golden as Devon butter from good living and there were bright amber glints in his brown eyes. They sat facing one another for a while and suddenly Fria bobbed her head quickly three or four times. The tiercel shuffled his feet, flicked his wings and lowering his head, neck outstretched, wailed softly.

For half an hour they sat watching one another and Fria made no sound. Then the tiercel abruptly launched himself from the tower and flew out across the parkland towards the edge of the woods. He climbed quickly into the sky and disappeared over the crest of the trees out of Fria's sight. With his going she wailed loudly and shifted around on her station restlessly, but she did not move from the tower. With a slightly raised head she watched the sky.

Ten minutes later the tiercel came back. Fria saw him at once. He hung a thousand feet above her and held something in his talons. He called to her, not wailing, but in a commanding *krak-krak-krak*. He flew directly over Fria holding a magpie he had taken from the far side of the wood. As he passed he dropped the bird.

Fria watched it fall in an untidy tumble of sprawling black and white plumage. It dropped into the rhododendron shrubberies a hundred yards from her. Fria made no movement and her immobility seemed to enrage the tiercel. He dropped from his pitch and dived at her, wailing and chattering to himself. He passed three feet above her, the wind of his passage ruffling her feathers, and then swung up, climbed high, and disappeared over the woods again.

Some minutes later the tiercel came back to his high station, holding a turtle dove. He dropped it for Fria and she ignored it as it fell through the gaping roof of the ruined house into the rubble below.

The tiercel dived, wailing plaintively at her again, and then disappeared down the long wooded slopes to the river.

He was gone for half an hour. Fria sat in the strengthening morning brightness. Flies buzzed in the ivy foliage below her and an early bumble-bee climbed awkwardly over the patches of stone-crop on the tower-roof. After a time Fria began to bob her head, shuffle her feet and wail softly to herself. She shook and aired her wings like a cormorant and then stabbed at a fly which settled on one of the bricks at her feet. For ten minutes she sat still and carven but her head was cocked slightly and her eyes watched the great segment of her vision for any sign of the tiercel.

She saw him when he was a mile away, flying high and coming down the river line from the opposite direction to the one which he had taken in leaving.

Fria wailed, bobbed her head and then flew off the tower. She beat up swiftly on a line to meet the tiercel. He saw her coming, swung away and began to ring up higher and higher above her. Fria followed him to a thousand feet and hung there. The tiercel was over another thousand feet above her. He circled easily, sitting over her, wailing and croaking to himself. Then the tiercel made a short stoop half-way down to Fria. As he flattened out at the bottom instead of throwing up, he dropped something from his right foot.

It was a sandpiper – one of the flock which the tiercel had disturbed earlier on and which he had taken two miles up the river. The dead sandpiper dropped lightly, the breeze against its loose wings and tail swinging and eddying it.

Fria watched it fall towards her. It passed twenty yards from her. As it dropped away below her she turned over and went down after it in a dive more than a sharp stoop. She turned under it, half rolled on her back and grabbed clumsily at it with both feet. She took it in her right foot, swung slowly on to an even keel and then began to fly down to the parapet of the ruined house. As she did so the tiercel wailed and called above her.

Fria settled on a stone slab and began to feed on the sandpiper, taking no notice of the tiercel above. After a few moments the tiercel came down and settled on a parapet block ten yards from her. He sat silently watching her as she fed. The courtship had begun.

*   *   *

When Smiler went up to Highford House that Saturday afternoon there was no sign of Fria. On the roof he found the remains of the sandpiper and knew it had been a fresh kill. He waited for an hour, hoping that Fria would return, and then went down the hill to the river and worked his way through the leafy tunnel in search of her, thinking she might be perched somewhere after taking a bath.

Two hours later he went back to Bullaybrook Farm by way of Highford House and was delighted to see Fria sitting on the tower-top. He went happily back to the farm.

Fria was alone and the tiercel had gone. An hour before Smiler had first arrived the tiercel had taken wing, circled over the ruins, and called to Fria. She had gone up to him, and the tiercel had led the way, climbing high and heading for the coast, the call of his birth eyrie working in him. But as they had passed high over the coastline at Morte Point, unused to the wide vista of sea that opened under her, Fria had turned back. The tiercel had followed her and, after circling her for a while, had led the way northwards again. Fria had followed and then half-a-mile out at sea had baulked and returned south. The maneuver was repeated three times, and on the last occasion Fria had resolutely headed south for Highford House. The tiercel had watched her go and then turned northwards by himself, flying high between white banks of cumulus clouds.

Fria now sat alone on her tower while Smiler made his way back to the farm. He was half-way down the hill when he saw the small white police mini-van pull away from the front gate. It came up the hill and stopped alongside him.

Grimble, the cheerful-faced policeman, leaned out and gave him a nod and a smile, saying, "Hullo, Samuel – been setting some rabbit snares?"

168

Smiler grinned back and said, "They're not worth poaching with all the mixy about."

"You'd rather have a nice bit of red hake, eh?"

Smiler knew by now that "red hake" was the country term for salmon that had been illegally netted or gaffed from the river. He said, "I wouldn't know how to go about it."

"Pull the other one. Jimmy Jago wouldn't be backward in teaching his own kin how to poach a salmon."

"Well, he never has."

Something about the man's manner put Smiler on the alert.

The policeman said, "Where is Jimmy these days, then?"

"I don't know. Somewhere up north with a fair, I think."

"So you haven't seen him for some time, then?" The man's voice was casual, but Smiler sensed that there was some real intent behind it.

Keeping to the strict truth – though if pushed his loyalty to Jimmy would have made him forsake that – Smiler said, "He hasn't been around the farm for weeks. Why do you ask?"

The policeman chuckled and said, "Because the parson isn't the only one who takes an interest in his parishioners. Very fond of Jimmy, I am. Always like to know how he's getting on and where he's to be found – if I should fancy a piece of nice red hake."

He winked at Smiler and drove on. But Smiler, who, in the last year had developed an ear for insincerity, and could see through a deliberate casualness, was not deceived. The police wanted Jimmy Jago. He wondered why. Then he told himself, "No business of yours, Samuel M. Forget it."

After supper he went up to his room and opened his Latin dictionary, but before he began to force himself to study he decided that he would much rather be learning the Romany gypsy language which the Duchess and Jimmy spoke together. No hope of that. Meanwhile there was the Latin waiting and, unless he made a good showing in the next few weeks, he knew the Duchess well enough to realize that he would get no holiday during Laura's visit. Gosh, that would be terrible.

He shut the thought from his mind and began to do the translation Mr. Samkin had set him . . . *Abhinc annos tres . . . Three years ago* . . . His mind wandered. "Three years ago, Samuel M.," he told himself, "you were thirteen and kicking around the streets of Bristol, pinching milk bottles off doorsteps and comics from shops and not a blind idea in your head of what was going to happen to you or what you wanted to do." He bit the end of his pen and stared out of the window at the night sky and wondered what he would be doing three years from now and then, on the point of sliding into daydreams, he jerked himself back and, groaning, got down to his Latin again.

*　　*　　*

At ten o'clock that night Maxie came out of his pine-bough hide. He stretched and did some toe-touching to take the stiffness from him. Then, pack on back, he went through the darkness down to the river. There was hardly a length of the river from this point to the sea where, either on one bank or another, trout and salmon fishermen had not made a pathway to move from one pool or fishing-beat to the next. Maxie drank from the river which had dropped ˙now to almost normal level and was clear of all spate colouring. Maxie moved quietly, a dark shadow following the river. He had twenty miles to go and all the night before him. There were a few high clouds but plenty of starlight to help him, and his eyes rapidly accustomed themselves to the gloom, and memory of past forays along the river served him well. He knew each bridge, each weir, each small road-crossing and he recalled the places where the railway hugged the river and the road the railway. So far as he could he kept on the left bank to avoid both. He rested once, sitting below the steep river-bank to smoke a cigarette and take a few sips from his brandy flask.

Sunrise he knew was somewhere around half-past six. At half-past five he reached Eggesford bridge and crossed the road a hundred yards back from the river, knowing that there would be a man on duty in the high-perched signal box at the level crossing by the station. Ten minutes later he was climbing the hill and reached the Highford House parkland. He knew Highford House and its tower well, though it had been ten years since he had seen them.

He climbed through the empty window which

Jimmy Jago had always used to leave the house, picked his way over the rubble and down a broken flight of steps to the old cellars under the house. His feet left prints in the thick dust on the steps. Grinning to himself he took his cap off and reached back and dusted the marks away behind him. It had taken Jimmy six months to pass information to him, principally by leaving notes around the fields and quarries where the prison parties worked, notes that were read and then swallowed at once. Jimmy, when he planned something, was always thorough.

Maxie, now safe from observation below ground, switched on his pencil torch and went along the passage which was littered with broken masonry blocks – some conveniently arranged long ago by Jimmy – so that he could use them as stepping-stones to avoid leaving traces. The passage took a right-angle turn and opened into what had once been a wine vault. Brick-arched bin recesses were cut into three sides of the vault. Maxie flicked his torch along them from left to right and counted. His light stopped on the fifth recess. The floor was covered with some broken planks and the section of an old door. Maxie lifted aside the door section. Underneath was a round manhole.

He raised the hinged manhole lid and shone his torch down a short run of iron ladder-way which led to the main sewer system. He climbed down the ladder and lowered the manhole cover, against which he had leaned the door section. The cover closed and the door section dropped with it and masked it.

At the foot of the ladder there was an open space, shaped like an inverted bowl, its sides and roof brick-lined. Regularly spaced around it were four entrance and exit tunnels about two feet high which in the years long past had conducted the house drainage and storm water away. The place now was dry and well ventilated by the tunnels that breathed air through broken manholes and ventilation shafts set in the outside walls.

In the domed chamber itself was a nondescript chair and a low canvas safari folding-bed with a pile of blankets and a pillow on it, and there were three boxes stacked agianst one of the walls close to a niche which held three candlesticks already fitted with new candles.

Maxie crossed to the candlesticks, lit them, and, leaving one in the niche, set the others on the boxes. At the back of the niche a plain white envelope was propped.

As the light from the candles grew stronger from a few minutes' burning, Maxie dropped his haversack on the chair and then took the envelope.

Sitting on the bed he opened the letter. Inside was a large single sheet of paper covered back and front with typescript. At the sight of the typescript Maxie smiled. Jimmy was a careful man. He would never had risked using his own handwriting. Maxie was sure that the typewriter he had used would have long ago been destroyed or sunk in some bog or river. One glance at the typing showed that it had been an old, well-worn machine. He knew, too, that nothing in this chamber could ever be traced to Jimmy. Oh, Jimmy was a loyal man and a careful one and when the fire burned in him trouble for a blood brother meant nothing . . . they had shared enough in their time.

Maxie sat and read the letter. It was long and full of instructions and cautions. Maxie read it all carefully, and to some paragraphs gave particular attention.

Nobody comes up here much, except the farm blokes and later maybe weekend picnic parties so you must stay fixed until after sunset. Can't say how long things will take once I know you're away from the moor, but will make short as poss and let you know next move which I'm already working on. . . .

. . . you've got food for over a month, water outside from roof, you'll see. Not likely to have a drought this time of year so no worry. . . .

If anything goes wrong and you have to run for it you must take a chance on you-know-who – and the climate isn't healthy there at the moment but I don't see you being turned away.

When he had finished reading the letter Maxie burnt it, and then set about making himself comfortable. He unpacked the stores from the boxes and sorted them and he blew out two of the candles. He might be a long time here and the light from one was enough for him. He whistled softly to himself as he moved around. The first stage was over. Everything now depended on Jimmy. The thought of having to live in the chamber for weeks and weeks gave him no qualms. After prison life it meant nothing. He would be free to leave it between sunset and sunrise. There were plenty of animals who lived a nocturnal life – now he had joined them.

*　　*　　*

Just after sunrise the next morning, as Fria was sitting on the tower-top, the tiercel returned. He flew high above her, circling and calling. Fria looked up, bobbed her head and did a little shuffling dance on the tower bricks, but she made no sound. The tiercel stooped and threw up ten feet above her head. As he shot skyward Fria called *kek-kek-kek*. The tiercel swung away down river and passed out of sight. Fria waited immobile on the tower and at ease, as though she knew he would be back, as though she knew that the desire in him to return to his old eyrie was weaker than the blood drive in him to find a mate.

She saw him as he came back, two thousand feet up. She launched herself from the tower and flew easily up to meet him. When she was five hundred feet below him he dropped a bird for her. It was a golden plover. As it passed by her Fria went down after it, caught it, and flew with it to a lower, thick branch of an oak on the edge of the wood, settled, and began to eat it.

The tiercel came down and sat two yards away from her on the outer end of the branch. He watched her eat. When she had finished Fria sat facing the tiercel. They watched one another, still as carved figures, while the Spring morning grew around them. After half an hour the tiercel suddenly wailed, stretched his wings high over his back and then flew off to the ruined house. Fria sat on the oak branch and watched him. He moved about the parapets and ruined roof of the house, exploring the niches and ledges, a restlessness driving him on. Often he was lost to Fria's sight. Sometimes he flew half-way back to her, wailed or called softly as though to entice her, and then turned back to the house again. He flew to the tower and worked his way over the leads and then dropped down to the recess ledge and shuffled inside. Fria made no move, but something of his restlessness and excitement was slowly communicated to her, though she gave no outward show of it.

Smiler came up to Highford House after lunch. There was no sign of Fria on the tower-roof. He climbed up to his favourite observation spot on the roof of the ruined house and began to search the surrounding countryside with his field-glasses.

Then, lying on his back and scanning the sky, he found Fria, and with her the tiercel. For a moment he could not believe his eyes and his hands trembled so much that the glasses shook and he lost both birds. Steadying himself by leaning backwards against a parapet stone, he picked them up again and a long sigh of pleasure broke from him as he realized that the thing he had longed for might have happened. "Samuel M.," he told himself, "don't be too sure, but . . . oh, let it be."

The tiercel was flying high above Fria, but

176

Smiler could see that it had to be a tiercel. It was much smaller than Fria and much faster. Above him both birds had long seen Smiler but were unconcerned with him.

As he watched now, Smiler was treated to one of the rare sights of Nature. The tiercel was giving a courting display of his powers to Fria. He stopped vertically and plunged a thousand feet down to Fria in less than seven seconds, threw up alongside her and soared high again in an angled, elongated figure of eight and rolled out of the bottom of the figure to dive at her again with rapid wing-beats and swing about her in a tight circle. For five minutes the tiercel cut and winged and dived and stooped, knifing his way into and out of figures and maneuvers with a terrifying mastery of flight. Fria circled on a steady pitch and gave no sign that the aerobatics meant anything to her. But down below Smiler held his breath in an agony of delight at the display, the sound of the tiercel's occasional wailing and calling and the air-hiss of his stoops coming faintly down to him. At the end of the display the tiercel winged up and, as though drawn after him by some irresistible pull, Fria rose too. In a few seconds both birds were gone, lost behind a slow-moving bank of clouds.

Smiler waited for the rest of the afternoon for them to return. He saw no sign of them, but he was not unhappy. He had a strong feeling that they would be back – but even if they did not come back he knew that he would still be happy because Fria with a mate would have found the life which was her true destiny. He climbed down from the

177

roof and went back to the farm with a light step, singing to himself.

Just before sunset the peregrines came back, flying in from the south together and landed on the recess ledge a yard apart to roost for the night.

When darkness was full, and the last of the Sunday traffic on the main road in the valley had thinned to an occasional car, headlights dusting the night with stiff, golden probes, Maxie came out from the house, drank from the water tank and filled a plastic container to take back down to the chamber with him. He stretched his arms and breathed the night air and then moved quietly away towards the shrubberies. Under the pale starlight, from their tower-top, the two peregrines saw him and watched unmoving. They were soon to know him and accept him as part of the night movement and sounds around them, Fria without concern, for she was used to human beings at close quarters, but the tiercel always with a sense of unease for the shape of man to him was the shape of danger.

*   *   *

In his diary that night Smiler wrote an account of the tiercel's coming, and finished:

> . . . and if he stays and they really mate they might make an eyrie on Fria's ledge and I could get to see the young ones. I might even be able to get up inside the tower sometime and see them through the brick gap, though I wouldn't

want to do nothing – bother, anything – what would scare them away.

Anyway, I'm glad for Fria she's got a husband. Crikeys! I'll have to find a name for him.

Saw Sandra and that Trevor as I came down the hill tonight. She made some daft remark and rolled her eyes at me – just to annoy Trevor really. Perhaps she'll stop all that nonsense after Laura's been. . . . Laura – hooray, hooray and three cheers.

9

↜ Family and Other Affairs ↝

The April days lengthened and for Smiler – who had now heard from Laura that she was definitely coming at the end of the month – often seemed unreasonably laggard in their passing. He worked hard on the farm and hard too at his studies – particularly Latin – because he was determined to get a week's holiday for Laura's visit.

Spring took the valley in days of boisterous winds and slashing rainstorms, and then changed mood to clear the skies and summon up balmy southerly breezes that made the hedgerows and meadows and woods alive with the spring fever of wild life and the spring thrust of growth. The adders and grass snakes found warm rock slabs on which to sun themselves, and the little green lizards scuttled in the stone rubble of Highford House. Primroses padded the lane-sides, violets and milkmaids made purple and lilac patterns in the fresh green of new grass, and the trees were hazed with leaf, except for the tardy oak. The dippers, kingfishers and the yellow and grey wagtails were nesting along the river, and with each fair rise of water the salmon and sea trout moved upstream. The larches were suddenly decked with the pale glow of new growth, and the voles, shrews and field mice built their nests and burrows and brought off their naked pink litters of shut-eyed young. The early wild daffodils already showed brown seeding-heads, and tulips flamed precociously in cottage gardens.

The Duchess sat in the entrance of her painted tent on fine afternoons but the silk cloth remained over her crystal ball. She had no desire to look into the future. She knew that Maxie must be at Highford House and, although she knew, too, that Smiler often went there, she had enough knowledge of Maxie to realize that he would never show himself to anyone. But, nevertheless, she could have wished that Smiler would not go there.

In Bristol Ethel nagged regularly about the letter Albert had for Smiler; and Albert could find no answer for her except that something would turn up.

The police all over the country, but particularly in Devon, were still keeping an eye open for Maxie.

And in more than one creature, human and otherwise, the restless drive of April was forcing new patterns of behaviour, not all of them sensible.

Trevor Green asked Sandra Parsons if, when his father bought him a farm of his own in a few years' time, she would marry him. Sandra refused to commit herself – not because she did not like him or thought the prospect unpleasant but because for the moment she had no intention of giving up one shred of her liberty to live each day as it came while she could. She said tantalizingly, "Anyway – who knows what can happen in three years? You're not the only pebble on the beach by a long chalk. A farmer's one thing, but I rather fancy I'd like to marry a doctor – or, perhaps, a vet. They've got more class." She knew perfectly well that Trevor Green had learnt that Smiler hoped to be a vet. one day.

Trevor Green, had he been a well-balanced young man, would have understood her teasing mood, but the idea was fixed in his head that Smiler was his rival, Smiler, who, he knew, was studying to be a vet., Smiler, too, a person who knew where he was going and was pretty sure to get there. Trevor Green wished Smiler in Timbuctoo, but since that couldn't be arranged, he just wished him ill and waited for a chance to promote it, large or small.

Up at Highford House, Maxie found himself – to his surprise – strangely restless in his new captivity. In simple terms it was not the captivity that irked him but the lack of work to feed his mind and body. In Princetown there had always been work and always – no matter how limited – company. And Maxie, who loved company, also had little time for idleness. The lack of these began to work on him, and there were days when he sometimes took the risk – out of sheer boredom– of leaving his safe chamber for a few minutes out in the sunshine and fresh air. It was from this need that he discovered the peregrines and found a great lift in his spirits from watching them now and then. He did this during the first hour of light on some fine mornings.

*   *   *

For the first two days after his return the tiercel hunted with Fria and, particularly when there was a good movement in the wind, would give his courtship displays. At other times he continued to creep into crevices of the roof structure of the ruined house and around the broken places in the brickwork of the tower, searching for a nesting-place and croaking and wailing at Fria to follow him.

Fria remained uninterested. But as the days went by two things happened to her. The first was that by hunting with him she learned to make her stoops steeper and faster and, either from chance or imitation as she watched his killing, learned to extend her rear talons and strike a bird cleanly and quickly to death. As far as flying ability was concerned, although she improved her skills vastly, she never reached the high degree of mastery which the tiercel had, never quite seemed to have the effortless and exuberant mastery of the air which was his, especially when there was a strong wind blowing. The second thing was that the tiercel's persistent, almost fussing, excitement around the tower and the house searching for a nesting-site eventually passed to her. She joined him, and the two of them spent long periods creeping and probing and testing likely places. Because these were few, there were times when the tiercel would fly off, perhaps hoping that Fria would follow him, to search for other places in the district. Fria showed no true interest, sliding away from him and turning back to Highford House after a while. She was tied to it, in memory possibly, as her true birthplace, her natural eyrie area, because it was here that she had become completely free and had made her first kills.

Always the tiercel came back to her and, eventually, his excitement shared fully by her now, Fria picked her spot – which was the recess that for so long had been her refuge. She fussed around it, scratching at the brick dust and eroding brick faces of its floor, lowering her breast to the ground and working a slight hollow which 't would fit. Now and again she would rest in the hollow in a brooding position. After a couple of days, the tiercel seemed to accept that this was her chosen spot. He gave up his search and would sit on the tower or the ruined house or sometimes on the top branch of the big oak on the wood's edge and wail and croak to her. One morning, early, and seen only by Maxie, Fria came out of the recess and flew to the rooftop and there the two birds mated as they would do daily afterwards until there were eggs in the tower recess.

Smiler missed their earlier matings but he saw later ones. The daylight was spreading further into the evenings now and on the days when he did not have to go to Mr. Samkin he walked up to Highford for an hour before settling to his studies in his room. He was well used to seeing the tiercel now and slowly the tiercel was getting used to seeing him. But the peregrine never sat on the tower-roof when Smiler was in his place on the housetop opposite. He would fly off to the great oak or ring up into the air and disappear. Fria would seldom follow him. Mostly she sat in the recess hollow and Smiler could just see the top of her head through his glasses.

One week-end towards the end of April Smiler

carried a work-bag up to Highford with a kit of tools. In the close-grown fir plantation behind the shrubberies he found a fallen fir tree with a sound trunk. He stripped the branches from it with a billhook and saw, and then cut regularly spaced notches along its length. Into these he fitted split lengths of branches, screwed home firmly with three-inch screws to form ladder rungs along the spine of the trunk. Waiting for a time when both peregrines were away from the tower, he carried the ladder inside and maneuvered it up the stair-case until he came to the gap. He wedged the butt end into a corner of the stairs and then lowered the top of the ladder across the gap and against the beginning of the higher flight of stone steps. By angling the ladder over the gap diagonally he managed to wedge it securely and then climbed up. He had no intention of trusting himself to the upper portion of the stairs whose broken base projected out over the gap. He found, however, that from the second rung from the top of the ladder he could stand up, using his hands against the inner tower wall for support, and just look through the hole in the bricks into the recess. He stood there the first time, legs trembling, balancing himself and hoping that nothing would slip.

The recess was far bigger inside than he had guessed it might be. The hollow that Fria had scooped for herself was clear to see. It was about two inches deep and completely bare. Scattered over the ground were a few dead twigs, a pigeon's iron-grey tail feather which Fria had carried up and idly dropped, and the bleached, frail bones of the skeletal frame of a small bird which had been one of Fria's very early kills.

Knowing now that with caution and by choosing his times he could observe the eyrie, Smiler started down the ladder. He was three feet down when its butt-hold gave way. The ladder slipped around a hundred and eighty degrees without losing its original slanting position. Smiler was spun round, his feet slipped from their rung and he just managed to hold on with his hands, hanging and swinging over a drop of thirty feet to the stone steps near the bottom of the tower. The moment of shock gone, he held tight with his hands and then found the strength in his back muscles and legs to draw his feet up under him and hook them over the nearest rung. He rested like that for a moment or two, the panic and fright easing from him, and then went slowly down the underside of the ladder, from rung to rung, dangling like a great sloth out for a leisurely excursion.

He reached safety and stood breathing hard. "Let that, Samuel M.," he told himself, "be a sharp lesson to you. The next time you come up you bring a cold chisel and hammer and make a hole in the stonework for a proper footing for the ladder."

He carried the ladder out of the tower and hid it in the shrubbery among clumps of dead bracken.

That evening while he was having supper the Duchess told him that she had met Mr. Samkin who had told her that there had been a vast improvement in his Latin. He could, she said, consider his holiday as good as a certainty. In addition Mr. Samkin would also let him off his study visits that week.

Then, before Smiler could thank her, she went on, "And when your Laura's gone you've got some serious thinking and deciding to do."

"I have, ma'am?"

"Yes, you have, Sammy."

"I don't understand you, ma'am."

For a moment she eyed him severely, fondling the ears of Scampi who sat in her lap. Then she said, "Oh, yes, you do, Sammy. Have you forgotten that so far as they're concerned you're in trouble with the police? Have you forgotten that somewhere off on the high seas you've got a father who most certainly would like to know what you're up to? You tell me you write to your sister and her husband, but they don't know where you are or much about what you're doing. I think you ought to tell them – in confidence. They won't let you down and they can write to your father——"

"You don't know my sister Ethel, ma'am, she——"

"I think it more likely that you don't know her. You approach her like a man and she'll treat you like one. You're not a small boy now whose ears she boxed for dirty hands and a runny nose and untidy habits." She grinned suddenly, and went running on, "Now don't start to fidget. I'm going to say what I'm going to say. You've got to do some straight thinking for yourself. You've got yourself nicely placed here, we all like you, you're working hard at your studies so you can get to take examinations, and you've got Laura coming, and

187

if you can get a spare hour or so you're off to Highford House after that blessed falcon of yours."

"Well, ma'am, I don't see anything wrong in that."

"And there isn't – except that it's not enough because you've got a shadow over you. And let me tell you, Sammy, that a lot of people in this world have shadows over them and really can't do anything about them. But you can."

"You mean about the police and all that?"

"That's what I mean."

"But I can't do anything about that." Smiler paused and eyed her closely. "I'm waiting for that pebble to drop. You told me, ma'am, that——"

"Whatever I told you didn't mean that you could sit on your bottom, do nothing and wait for it to drop. It'll drop when you do the right thing."

"Which is what, ma'am?"

The Duchess shook her head, her red curls bouncing. "You're sixteen and a half. That's old enough, Sammy, to figure out almost any problem for yourself. Let me say this, innocence is a light in the eyes which reasonable people can always recognize."

Smiler understood her perfectly, but he said despairingly, "But I couldn't give myself up to the police now. Besides . . . it might get you into trouble for having me."

The Duchess chuckled. "You freckle-faced, blue-eyed devil – you don't twist me like that. You let me handle any troubles that might come to me. I'll give you until Laura has gone to think it over. Now off with you and get your nose in your books – and begin to think about what I've said."

But after Smiler had gone the Duchess sat on and knew in her heart that she had been motivated by more than Smiler's interests. She wanted him away from Highford House. Every time he went up to the place there was the risk of danger, of the odd turn of Fate's dice which could alter the lives of many people.

*   *   *

In his diary that night, Smiler wrote:

At supper tonight the Duchess gave me a blowing up about things. I can see why in a way. Fact, I suppose she's right, but I'm darned if I'm going to think about it until Laura's gone. Might ask her about it. Blimey – walking into the police and giving myself up! Funny about the Duchess. I think she's missing Jimmy a lot or got something on her mind.

Nearly killed myself on the tower ladder today. Saved by a Tarzan act. Me Tarzan – you Laura. Ha-ha!

*   *   *

On the Monday of the last week in April the falcon Fria laid her first egg. Its shell was a dull white marked with reddy-brown and some violet blotches. The next day she laid another, and a third on the following day. After that she laid no more and started to brood and, at first, she was content to share some of this task with the tiercel. By this time, too, Smiler had made his ladder fastening secure. When he managed to slip up to Highford on the Tuesday for half an hour before supper he put the ladder in position while the two peregrines were away from the tower. When he saw the eggs he nearly fell off the ladder again with delighted surprise. But as he put the ladder away amongst the bracken he decided firmly that he would not use it again for fear of disturbing Fria or the tiercel until there were young birds in the nest. He knew from his reading that once the full clutch was laid and the falcon began to brood in earnest that it would take twenty-eight or a few more days for the incubatory period to be completed. So the ladder lay in the bracken and the new growths raised their green crozier heads around it.

A week before Laura arrived Fria was sitting steadily. At first the tiercel had shared some of the brooding with her so that she could go off and hunt, but as the days went by Fria sat more and more tight on the eggs. The tiercel began to kill for her. Twice a day, in the early morning and late evening, he would come back from his forays and, hanging high over the great oak at the wood's edge, would call to her. Fria would come out and catch the kill which he dropped. Sometimes she would eat it on the oak branch but more often as the days went by would take it to the tower-top where, standing on the leads, she could eat without being seen because she was hidden by the brickwork of the crenellated parapet that decorated the summit of the tower. At first, too, she would sometimes fly down to the river to drink and bathe. But later she was content to fly down to the edge of Maxie's water-tank and drink from that, and her bathing became very rare.

With Fria sitting steadily, the tiercel often left her for long periods after he had fed her. In time he knew the river valley and its surroundings for miles north and south of Eggesford. And quite a few people came to know him. The water bailiff, standing quietly and hidden under the overhang of some trees, saw him come down one day over a stretch of reed and iris-thick swamp and take a mallard drake as it was planing down to the marsh. The tiercel carried it to a gravel spit in the middle of a fast, shallow run of the river not twenty yards from him. He stood like a statue for half an hour watching the peregrine feed. A few visitors to the Fox and Hounds Hotel saw the tiercel flying high but a lot of them failed to recognize his breed. But some of them did and most of them kept quiet about what they had seen. But the presence of the peregrines inevitably became more remarked and the rumour of their whereabouts began to spread slowly . . . a little trickle of news and speculation amongst local people and visitors, a trickle which, blocked here, would seep along some new channel.

Away from Eggesford the tiercel was shot at twice. Once by a young man from Barnstaple – who had driven out for a day's poaching with an unlicensed shotgun – as the tiercel swooped round a corner of a wood chasing a pigeon; and another time by a farmer, walking gun in hand along the edge of a field of young corn. The tiercel who had been feeding at the foot of the hedge flew up as the man crested the rounded swell of the field and came into view. Instinctively he had brought up the gun and fired. A few pellets from the outer spread of the shot pattern rattled against the tiercel's left wing harmlessly. The farmer, who was not by nature an intolerant man, watched the tiercel fly away, recognized the bird late for what it was, and was thankful that he had missed it.

Luckily, so far, no one had discovered that there was a pair of peregrines in the district and that their eyrie was in the red brick tower at Highford House.

*　　*　　*

Laura arrived on the late afternoon train from Exeter at Eggesford Station. Smiler had been waiting for half an hour. Not because the train was late but because he had arrived early. With his own money he had hired a car from a local garage, and the garage proprietor sat in it now outside the station, grinning to himself at the excitement which Smiler – whom he knew – had been unable to suppress. Jerking up and down on his seat as though t'were full of pins, he thought. Must be a girl. Can't be nothin' else but a girl.

Inside the station Smiler walked up and down the platform restlessly. He wore a new pair of trousers, a freshly ironed blue shirt with a bold red tie, and a slightly over-sized green and blue-checked jacket which Bob – who did a little second-hand trading on the side – had sold him at a bargain price, pointing out, "Never mind the fit, lad, you'll grow to it in a month. Look at the material. Genuine West of England cloth and a bargain at a quid." His fair hair was bound down close to his scalp with a liberal anointment of some violet-smelling hair lotion which had been left behind by Jimmy Jago. "From the days," had said the Duchess, "when he found it in his fancy to do a little serious courting but soon thought better of it."

The sparrows and starlings quarrelled on the station roof as Smiler paced up and down. Across the tracks below the bank a man was fly-fishing in the pool under the bridge. Smiler watched him, relishing the smooth parabolas of the line's movement, and remembered the one and only time that he had caught a salmon on a fly and how he would never have landed it but for Laura's advice.*

He heard the rattle of the train when it was a quarter of a mile away and then the challenging, bugle-like notes as it hooted for the level crossing and the station. As the train rolled to a stop alongside the platform Smiler stood rooted to the spot with a sudden trembling in his legs and a hard dry lump in his throat, watching the few passengers descend.

Dismay swept over him as they all disembarked and moved towards the station exit. Laura was not with them. Loose brown hair, brown eyes and a sun-tanned skin. . . . Gosh, he thought, perhaps after all this time I've forgotten what she looks like. Panic rose slowly in him.

A voice from behind him said, "Well, you dafty, aren't you going to give me welcome?"

* *Flight of the Grey Goose.*

193

Smiler turned. Standing beside him, case in hand, was a tallish young woman, her long brown hair tied in a pony-tail, wearing a red trouser suit that fitted her slim body as though it were another skin, a flash of white silk scarf at her throat, white, wedge-heeled shoes on her feet, and a smile on her lips which were made up with dark red lipstick.

"Laura! Gosh, I didn't recognize you!" He grabbed at her hand and began to work it like a pump handle.

"Well, thanks, Sammy. That's aye a gay welcome to Devon. And did you think, you loon, that I'd come wearing my farm or boat clothes? And when you've finished with my hand I'll have it back and you can give me a kiss. It's all right – don't fret – the stuff's kiss-proof." Her eyes shining, she leaned forward and Smiler kissed her, his head swimming so much that for a moment Laura put up a hand to stop him pushing her backwards.

"Oh, Laura," cried Smiler, "you look super! You're so grown up!"

"It's a thing that happens – but you don't have to shout it to the whole world. And you've not done so bad yourself. You've filled out and you're taller. And, my goodness, laddie, have you become a smart dresser. Where did you get all this gear?" She fingered the loose sleeve of his jacket.

"From one of the Ancients."

Laura laughed, leaned forward and kissed his cheek, saying, "That doesn't surprise me. Never mind, things will seem different when we get into jeans." Then, spontaneously, she hugged his arm and went on, "Oh, it's good to see you, Sammy!"

"And me, you, too. Here, give me that." He grabbed her case and, hurrying her along the platform, went on, "I've got a car waiting, hired it myself, and the driver's the garageman, and he says he grows the most marvellous dahlias and he's got a cat that keeps biting out its own fur and eating it so I said I'd look it up in one of my vet. books and see what I could do about it, and – Crikeys! I forgot to ask. Are your mother and father well?"

"Aye, they send their love. And my father's a few pounds poorer by way of my rail fare and so's my mother because of this." Laura fingered her red suit.

And the car driver, seeing them coming, hopped out of the car quickly to take the case and stow it away, and said to himself that although he had known it must be a girl, *this* was a girl that could make both a man's eyes pop out on first meeting unless he blinked fast to keep them in.

Driving them back to the farm, the garageman eyed them in his mirror as they sat in the back holding hands and, because a silence had descended on them that he thought might freeze them up forever, grinned and said to Laura, "You're the best-looking number, miss, that I've ever picked up from Eggesford and there've been one or two movie stars among them." Then with a wink, he went on, "Sammy here didn't tell me he had such a good-looking sister!" At that they all laughed and, somehow from that moment, the strangeness was gone from the two and they were Laura and

Smiler and the months of separation dissolved like a river mist under the first warm rays of the sun.

From that moment began the happiest week that Smiler could remember for years and years – which was not strictly true, but understandable, for the memories of the young are short.

The Duchess took to Laura as though she were one of her own daughters, and a favourite one at that. And Laura took to the Duchess and knew at once that the red curls were no wig, and she helped with the cooking and in the kitchen as though she had lived in the house for years. The whole building was a babble of chatter and laughter and happiness which – when the two were away from the place – the Duchess would sit back and think about, sighing to herself with a mixture of quiet joy and nostalgia.

The Ancients, because they wanted to and also because they knew it teased Smiler, brought Laura a posy every morning when they came to work – not a posy between them, but one each. They mock-quarrelled with one another as to which was the best, making Laura give a decision which she did, meticulously keeping the score even but wondering what she would do on her last day which would be an odd one. She need not have worried because the Ancients – as it turned out – knew better than to embarrass a lady. On the last day they brought a double-sized one between them. And, from the depths of the stone barn, they hauled out a girl's bicycle which Jimmy was – or had been – hoping to refurbish and sell one day. They put it in order and Laura was free to roam the countryside with Smiler on his bicycle, both of them in working denims and shirts and Smiler's haversack loaded with a lunch provided by the Duchess.

One lunchtime Smiler took Laura into the bar of the Fox and Hounds and, while she drank cider, he had a glass of beer because he felt it was a more manly, grown-up thing to do when Laura was with him. But the gesture was spoiled when she said, "You don't have to make such a face drinking it and from what I remember of you, you had a giddy enough head from a drop of cider without taking to beer." When Smiler protested and they quarrelled happily, the barman, Harry, came over. Winking at Laura, he said, "If he's giving you trouble, miss, just say the word and I'll throw him out."

But there were to be serious moments between the two during that week. The first came when Smiler took Laura up to show her his room and tell her all about his studies and about the peregrines up at Highford House, and a dozen other things. As he was talking Laura touched the little clay model of Johnny Pickering and said, "What's this, Sammy?"

Smiler told her, and her face grew serious.

She said, "Coming from where I do, I won't say that kind of magic doesn't work, but there's times when a body has no call to depend too much on it."

"What can you mean?"

Laura smiled. "I'll tell you when I have the mind. Right now you can walk me down this

Bullay brook of yours. There's daylight for an hour yet."

They walked down the brook for a mile, and sat on the edge of a deep pool where, as the dusk thickened, a sea trout jumped and the small brook trout dimpled the water film as they fed from a drifting hatch of stone flies. The pipistrelle bats cut the darkening sky above them with fast and erratic wing-beats. Because their ears were young, they could catch the thin high notes of the bats talking to one another. After a while the talk between them ceased. Smiler held Laura's hand and, a little later, Laura laid her head against his shoulder. They rested there in the slow vibrant bliss of their reunion while the world darkened softly around them. Suddenly from the thickets on the other side of the brook a nightingale began to sing – which was no surprise because for the right people nightingales have a wonderful sense of timing.

That night Smiler wrote in his diary:

Laura's here, and gosh I don't know whether I'm on my head or my heels. She's more lovely than what I remembered her like – and just as cheeky and bossy which is super. Super. Super Laura. The peregrines tomorrow. (I am going to get a box with a key and lock this diary up from now on.)

*   *   *

The next morning as the first light touched the high wood crest behind Highford House, Maxie who had been stretching his legs with a walk came back to the house. He was reluctant to go down to his chamber and stood for a moment in the shadowed angle of a buttress by his water tank. The dawn chorus was in full song and the thickets and shrubberies were alive with bird movement. He watched a kestrel come across the field from the big chestnut and hover over the old garden below the tower. Maxie smiled to himself as the tiercel – who had passed the night on the tower-top – suddenly launched himself downwards and chased the kestrel away, racing and swerving after it with rapid wing-beats. The kestrel dived into the top branches of an old crab-apple tree by the wood and screamed at the tiercel as it went by.

Keep off my patch, thought Maxie. As the tiercel came back and settled on the tower Maxie nodded upwards to the bird. Good for you old man, he thought. You look after what's yours. A missus and soon you'll have kids. You're lucky. Oh, yes, lucky.

He turned away and climbed through an empty window into the house and made his way to his vaulted chamber, memory plaguing him, and impatience growing in him because he had waited long now and had had no word from Jimmy Jago.

Two hours later Smiler and Laura arrived at Highford. Smiler helped Laura to climb to the roof and they sat on the parapet together watching the tower. The tiercel was nowhere to be seen. Through the glasses they could just see the top of Fria's head as she brooded her eggs in the recess. After about fifteen minutes, from high overhead, came a long drawn call of *wickoo-wickoo*. A thousand feet up the tiercel circled.

"He's brought her food. You just watch," said Smiler. As he spoke Fria shuffled out to the lip of the ledge, raised her head, shook her loose feathers into trim and flew off, rising with a slow flapping movement until she was well above the old oak. From high above her the tiercel dropped the jackdaw which he had taken as it flighted between two clumps of fir plantations. The bird fell slowly and Fria with quickening wing-beats flew up and under it, rolled over as it passed her, and came down in a short stoop and seized it.

She dropped down and flew under the green canopy of the old oak and settled on her feeding-branch. The tiercel circled for a while and then, half closing his wings, came down fast to the tower. He pulled out of his dive, wings open, hanging for a moment above the recess ledge and then settled on the lip. He shook his plumage firm and sat on guard until Fria should have finished her meal.

Laura watched him through the field-glasses. He sat full in the light of the morning sun which caught the bright yellow cere at the base of his strong blue-black beak, a bold glare in his eyes. His dark-crowned head and the darker streaks of his cheek and moustache stripes and the steely shine of his back and wings were like the armoured accoutrements of some arrogant, feudal knight.

She said with a touch of awe in her voice, "Oh, Sammy, isn't he the bonny bird? He looks like some noble prince in armour ready to fight to the death for his lady."

From that moment for both of them, the tiercel was named and became the Prince. Twenty minutes later Fria came back from her meal and the tiercel Prince dropped from the tower and beat away fast and low down the slopes of the parkland to disappear near the river.

Smiler said, "He's away to the river for his morning bath."

They climbed down from the house and Smiler showed Laura the ladder he had made, explaining that he was not going to use it again until he was sure that the eggs had hatched.

They went back to their bicycles and rode off to go to Barnstaple. Laura wanted to do some shopping for presents to take back to her father and mother and friends, having said that morning to Smiler, "I know you don't want to waste time shopping in a town but it's got to be done – so we might as well get it over and then you won't be fussing about it for the rest of the week."

It rained hard that afternoon. To escape it they went to a cinema and sat at the back, holding hands, and Smiler when he came to write up his diary that night could not remember even the name of the film they had seen.

He wrote:

The tiercel is the Prince. Laura named him after one look, bang on the nose. Had to take some eggs up to the village after supper from the D. to Mr. Samkin. Laura stayed behind nattering to the D. Glad she did, really. Not very keen about Sandra seeing us because you never know

201

what she's going to say just out of devilment. Come to think of it both Sandra and Laura like doing that. Mr. Samkin asked about Fria and I told him about Prince. I got a feeling that he already knew there was a tiercel up there. Shouldn't be surprised if he is already paying a visit now and then to Highford. He's a quiet one, but he's all right. I wish the teachers at my stinking old school had of been like him.

What Smiler did not write in his diary was that coming away from Mr. Samkin's he had run into Sandra who had said, "I hear tell that you've got your girl-friend staying at the farm for a week."

"Don't be silly," Smiler had said indignantly. "She's not my girl-friend. She's just some relation of Jimmy Jago's and I'll be glad when she's gone so she isn't tagging along all the time."

Sandra tossed her fair hair and grinned.

"The only time I saw her tagging along you had a grin on your face like a Cheshire cat that had taken all the dairy cream."

"If you think that, you ought to get your eyes tested."

As he cycled back down the hill Smiler thought, with a moment's crossness, that it was a funny thing that some people couldn't keep their noses out of other people's business. But by the time he got to the bottom of the hill he was saying to himself, "Samuel M., you didn't handle that right. You should have just told the straight truth. Maybe that would have put her off for good."

10

➳ *The Moment of Decision* ➳

If the time of waiting for Laura's arrival had passed snail-slow for Smiler, the days of her week in Devon appeared to race by. High pleasure seemed, like a glutton, to bolt and swallow the hours voraciously. They visited Highford at least once every day. Laura was disappointed that she would not be there when the young arrived, but she made Smiler promise to write and give her all the news of them when they showed. They cycled for miles around the countryside, fished for trout in the Bullay brook, went now and again for a lunchtime drink at the Fox and Hounds, and explored the river for miles up and downstream – and, by skilful maneuvering, Smiler managed to keep Laura away from the village and Sandra.

The morning of the day before Laura was due to go back, they walked the Bullay brook to the point where it ran into the Taw. They sat on a high bank overlooking the main river. A hundred yards downstream a heron stood in the shallows, fishing. A black mink ran along the far bank, scented them, raised its head, gave them a beady stare, and then turned back along its tracks and disappeared. A salmon jumped in the pool above them, bored with the long wait ahead until spawning time. A solitary early Mayfly hatched from the water. It drifted away on the film with raised wings to take the risk of a few moments' peril from lurking trout before it could lift itself into the air to its all too brief freedom.

Lying on his back in the grass, Smiler said, "I can't believe you're going tomorrow. Where's all the time gone?"

Laura was silent for a while, and then she said, "Sammy, I got something to tell you."

Smiler rolled over on his elbow and looked at her. A small, serious frown creased her suntanned brow.

"Well, what?"

"Well, before I left home my mother told me there was something I had to do."

"What was that?"

"Well, she knew from me that although you were writing to your sister and her husband that you hadn't told them where you were – except in Devon somewhere. And she felt that was all wrong. And . . . well, since I knew where they lived in Bristol from you, she said I had to go and see them on the way down and tell them where you were."

Smiler sat up quickly. "You did that?"

"Yes. I stopped off in Bristol. And it's a good thing I did. They're both very nice and I like them."

"Albert's all right. But my sister Ethel – you don't know her. If she takes a mind to it she'll be off to the police and – oh, Laura, why did you do it?"

"Stop panicking like a loon. Your sister won't do anything of the kind. They both promised me that before I exactly told them. And then . . . well, they gave me this for you."

Laura took an envelope from her pocket and handed it to Smiler.

Smiler recognized the writing on the envelope at once. It was his father's.

"It's from Dad."

"Yes, I know. Your Albert said you had to have it urgently, but he'd no way of sending it to you."

Smiler turned the letter over. "You know what's in it?"

"Of course not. I don't open people's letters. But from what Albert told me your father had written to him I do know that it's some good advice. And that's something that some folk – not a hundred miles from here – don't take to too gladly. Why don't you open it and see?"

Smiler opened the letter. It was a long letter in which his father explained what had happened to him to cause him to miss his ship, and how things had gone from then on, and a lot of chatty stuff about his doings. Reading it Smiler had a vivid picture of his father and his memory rioted with all the good things they had done together in the past – but all that was washed from his mind as he read the last paragraph:

. . . Well now – to the real thing, Samuel M. I know from Albert and the police reports that the company sent me about most of your goings on. But the thing is – no matter how you've been able to look after yourself (and I'm really proud about that) – you've got the wrong end of the stick. O.K. so you didn't pinch the old girl's bag and you ran away from that place they sent you. But that wasn't the thing to do and it no more is the thing to keep on doing. I don't know when I'll be back, but that makes no difference cos I should only make you do what you really ought to have done – if you'd used your noddle – long ago, and that's walk up to the nearest copper and give yourself up. The police aren't fools. The fact you run away tells them something was wrong, and the fact of giving yourself up will just make it more so. I'm not going to start sparking off and giving you orders. I know my Samuel M. All I know is that you got my advice – not orders – and I'll know you'll do the right thing. O.K?

Yours from the bottom of the world, but hoping to be home soon – lots of love, Dad.

P.S. They tell me you want to be a vet. That's fine – but you can't really settle to that until everythings cleared up, can you? Chin up.

Love again, Dad.

Silently Smiler handed the letter to Laura. As she read it he looked around him, at the sunlit river, and the green fields and the wood-sweeps of the valley-side. Above the high crest of the firs that hid the Highford hilltop from him he saw a handful of rooks sporting in the air, and far above them a pair of buzzards circling slowly on their broad wings. Fria and Prince were up there somewhere, Fria for certain would be sitting on her three eggs and in a couple of weeks they might be hatched. . . . All this and his work with Mr. Samkin and his pleasant billet with the Duchess to be thrown away, to be walked away from, perhaps for good, just because his father . . . A lump rose in his throat and he screwed his face muscles up to stop unwelcome tears seeping into his eyes.

Laura handed the letter back to him. "Your father's a fine and sensible man. Wronged you've been, but you've done nothing for yourself by running away. Oh, Sammy – I've told you that before."

Stubbornly Smiler said, "I never robbed that old lady – and I'm not giving myself up to the police."

Laura eyed him silently for a while and then she smiled and said, "You've got the letter. You know what your father thinks. I'm saying no more. It's no place of mine to tell you what to do. A man must make his own decisions. So, Sammy, I'm saying no more about it."

"But it means leaving the Duchess, and the peregrines, and all my studying and ——"

"No, Sammy," Laura interrupted him and stood up. "I don't want to hear anything about it. I know what you'll do. Now come on, let's walk up the river and have a bar snack at the Fox and Hounds and I can say goodbye to Harry."

And so it was that the subject was not mentioned between them again until a few moments before Laura got into the train at Eggesford to begin her journey home.

Smiler gave her a kiss and a hug and then took from his pocket a sealed envelope and handed it to her.

"Don't open it now, Laura. In the train. It's for you. It's a kind of present. Well, two presents." He grinned suddenly. "You brought me a letter – now you got one to take back with you."

The porter came by them and, winking, said, "Come on now, miss. Can't hold the train up. Parting is such sweet sorrow – but there's always another time and nothing stops the grass growing."

The train pulled out of the station and Laura waved from the carriage window until the curve of the line hid her. Smiler waved back, and two thousand feet above Fria's tower the tiercel caught the red flick of his bandana handkerchief and soared higher to chase a solitary buzzard, teasing it with short, playful, mock stoops.

In the carriage by herself Laura opened the envelope. Inside was a letter and a small silver chain necklace with a little silver fish hanging from it.

The letter read:

I got it in Barnstaple that day for you to wear and remember our promise for one day. I hope you like it.

I hope you'll like the second present too what is that I've made up my mind to do it.

Lots of love for ever, S.

Laura fixed the chain round her neck with tears in her eyes. Back at the station Smiler went out to the hired car. The garage man opened the door so that Smiler could sit alongside him. Seeing his long face, he grinned and said, "It ain't the end of the world, you know. But if it is, we can go back over Kersham bridge. I'll pull up so you can jump into the river and end it all. Knew a chap who did that once. Summertime it was, though, and the river dead low. Broke his leg on a rock."

*   *   *

Two days later Smiler finished work early and went up to Highford House. He sat for an hour on the roof. Fria was sitting tight on her eggs. The tiercel, Prince, was nowhere to be seen until five minutes before Smiler left. Suddenly he came down from the high blue sky in a vertical stoop over the tower. Fifty feet above it he threw up in a great figure of eight, the sound of his stoop and maneuver making the air sing. Then he rolled over and dived at the roof of the house. He passed two feet above Smiler – as though, Smiler thought, he knew it was goodbye and this was his way of saying it – and then landed with a quick back flicking of wings on the tower-top. Smiler saw the movement of Fria's head in the recess and heard her call quietly to the tiercel.

He climbed down from his roof perch and made his way back through the woods, looking at his wrist-watch to check the time because he knew exactly when the little police patrol car would be coming up Bullay brook hill.

As he loitered down the hill the car came over the brook bridge, passed the farm and began to climb the hill. Smiler raised a hand and the car pulled in by him.

With a broad smile on his red face Grimble, the policeman, said, "Hullo, Samuel. Your girl-friend's gone, I hear."

"Yes," said Smiler glumly. For a moment or two he felt his courage ebbing from him and he had a sudden desire to turn and run away. Then he thought of his father and of Laura and the whole of his future and he suddenly stammered out, "I got to tell you something. . . . You see . . . well, I want to be a police . . . I mean ——"

The policeman grinned. "If you want to be a policeman, you'll have to wait. You're not old enough yet."

"No, no, I don't mean that. I mean, I'm wanted by the police."

For a moment there was silence between them and then the man said, "Say that again."

"I'm wanted by the police. I'm a sort of . . . well . . . criminal, and I want to give myself up and get it over to really prove I didn't do it, and then I can be clear with my father and Laura and . . . well, and then get on with my studies. So you'd better take me back with you."

The policeman considered this and then said calmly, "Well, now – this all sounds very sudden and serious. A criminal, eh? Sort of on the run, you mean?"

"That's right." It was funny, Smiler thought, but he was feeling easier now as though for days he had been all stuffed up with . . . well, like with overeating, and now suddenly he was back to normal and really feeling good. He went on, "You see I escaped from approved school way back early last year and I got this place working on a farm in Wiltshire and then things went wrong there and then I went to the Laird in Scotland and then again things went wrong and ——"

"Now, hang on." The policeman smiled. "This sounds as though it's going to be a long story. I think we ought to go down to the farm and go into all this with the Duchess." Then, with a twinkle in his eyes, he said, "You wouldn't describe yourself as a dangerous criminal, would you?"

"No, of course not."

"Good. Then I won't put the handcuffs on you. Come on, hop in – and let's see if we can get this cleared up."

So they went down to Bullaybrook Farm and in to the Duchess who, the moment she saw them together, had a shrewd idea of what might have happened because Laura – in strict confidence – had mentioned Smiler's father's letter, and it had been clear that Smiler had something on his mind for the last few days. The Duchess produced cider and biscuits for the policeman, Mr. Grimble. His wife had had her fortune told more than once by the Duchess who had – the last time – accurately foretold that their fourth expected child would be a girl – which it was to Mrs. Grimble's delight. All the others were boys, "little hellions", she called them.

Smiler told the policeman his story, sticking only to the main facts. When he had finished, P.C. Grimble stroked his plump chin, took a sip of his cider, looked from Smiler to the Duchess and then, as though producing a great pearl of wisdom, said, "Interesting. Very interesting."

Smiler said, "If you're going to take me away, can I have a little while to pack some things?"

P.C. Grimble nibbled at a biscuit and then said, "Well, now, let's think about that. There's a lot of things I'll have to go into with my Super, and then we'll have to get on to the Bristol police and so on. All takes a little time and it's half-past seven now and my supper's waiting at home. Then, too, you *have* given yourself up so you *aren't* likely to change your mind about it – I hope?"

"No, sir."

"Well then, what I'm going to do is put you in the charge of the Duch – I mean, Mrs. Jago, here, until I get proper instructions, maybe tomorrow. So what I suggest now, Sammy, is that you go on up to your room and get on with a little studying, so that Mrs. Jago and me can have a quiet talk."

With a smile the Duchess, giving the nape of Smiler's neck an affectionate squeeze, pushed him gently and said, "Off with you."

When they were left alone together P.C. Grimble, "He's got guts."

"He's got more than that."

"Seems to me pretty certain he didn't do it. But that won't stop the trouble. I mean, you've had him here, harbouring as they say, and you knew all about him, and you put it around he was a nephew or something."

"Yes, I did – and I'd do it again. And so would a lot of other people who've also helped him, knowing all about him. Don't you worry about me. All my life trouble has risen with the sun for me most days. It's like an old friend now. I'd miss it."

"Well, yes. . . . Anyway, I don't suppose they'll make much of it. We're reasonable people, you know. Jimmy brought him from Scotland – that right?"

"Yes."

"Where is Jimmy these days?"

The Duchess shrugged her shoulders. "I doubt if I looked into my crystal I could find out. He goes with the wind. The family wanderlust runs hard in him."

"Like it does in Maxie Martin."

"What would you expect?"

"Seems like Maxie's got clear away."

"I suppose so."

"Mistake putting him in Princetown. He knows the moor and all this country like the back of his hand." Mr. Grimble shook his head, drained his cider and, rising, said, "But he'll never make it. They never do, you know. He'll get picked up one day. The boy's got the right idea finally. You can't go on running away from your rightful troubles. Face 'em."

"You preach a good sermon, and I agree with you."

The policeman grinned, reaching for his peaked cap, and said, "And there's plenty of things you could tell me – without looking into any old crystal ball. But you know me, I do my job but I don't go around bullying my neighbours about their business unless they ask for it. Well, I'll let you know about the boy soon's I hear."

*   *   *

Upstairs in his room Smiler sat at his work-table, an English grammar book open and neglected before him. On the mantelshelf the little clay figure of Johnny Pickering stood, shoulders bowed with the burden of the pebble on them. Through the window he saw the quick lightning-blue streak of a kingfisher flash down the brook. A pied fly-catcher flirted from the top of a laburnum tree in the garden and took an early moth. One of the few horses left at keep, rolled in the meadow on its back then righted itself and shook its black mane. A kestrel hovered on the far side of the stream, wing-tips lightly pulsing as it watched the move-ment of a field mouse foraging in the long grass.

Suddenly Smiler gave a deep sigh and pulled his diary out of the table drawer.

He wrote:

I've done it. And right afterwards I felt good about it. But, gosh, now I feel awful.

More than those few lines he had not the heart and spirit to write. At that moment his world was upside down. At that moment, too, in a seaport in Wales Mr. Jimmy Jago, sitting in his car, was penning his last threatening message to Johnny Pickering. It read – THE SANDS OF TIME ARE RUNNING OUT AND YOU KNOW WHAT YOU HAVE TO DO. At that moment, too, in his hiding-vault at Highford House Maxie Martin – worried that something might have happened to Jimmy Jago – made a decision that unless he had news from him within the next fortnight he would have to take action on his own.

At supper that evening Smiler said to the Duchess after a long silence, "I had to do it, ma'am, because of the letter from my father. But I'm sorry to make trouble for you, ma'am."

"What trouble, Sammy?"

"Well, about me being your nephew and you having me here knowing everything."

"Don't give it another thought, Sammy. The police won't bother about any of that." She smiled. "If they did they'd have too many people on their hands collecting everyone who has known about or helped you since you went on the run."

After supper Smiler went out to the barns because he felt that if the police came for him the next day he ought to pay a farewell visit to the animals. Actually, except for the farm creatures, there were very few boarding or circus animals left. The chimpanzee was there but he was going in a week, but the griffon and the mynah birds were gone and so was the barbary ram, the honey bear, and the tapir. The Duchess, Smiler had the feeling, had slowly turned against having caged animals, and she and the Ancients were now concentrating more on ordinary farming. They still took the horses, but that was different, Smiler thought, because they weren't caged up like the others. Freddie, the chimpanzee, shuffled to the front of his cage. Smiler scratched his head and then wandered round the few other cages that held boarders, his heart heavy. In a few days now he could be back in that approved school and all his freedom over the past year would have meant nothing. . . . Then he checked himself. "No," he told himself, "you got it wrong, Samuel M. Without all that you'd never have met Laura, Laura above all, and all the other people you've made friends with. And you wouldn't have known you wanted to be a vet."

He slept badly that night, waking on and off and lying in the dark, listening to the sound of the running brook, the occasional screech of a little owl – and twice the eerie churring notes of a nightjar.

The next day dawned with a change in the weather. The sky was full of low cloud and driving rain and Smiler went about his farm work waiting for the call from the Duchess that the police had arrived for him. But there was no visit or word from them that day.

But the following day P.C. Grimble called and said that the Bristol police were making enquiries. In the meantime they had passed a strict order that Samuel Miles was not to leave Bullaybrook Farm.

The next day, as Smiler was helping Bob to cut grass for silage in one of the lower valley meadows, Bill came into the field and said that Smiler was wanted at the farm right away.

Smiler said, "Is it them?"

Bob and Bill, who knew all about his trouble by now, looked at one another and then Bill said, "Well, there's a big black car in the drive."

Smiler said, "It's bound to be the police. I'd better say goodbye."

Bob shook his head. "Don't rush your fences, Sammy. It could be a lawyer to tell you your rich uncle's died in Australia and left you a fortune."

Smiler grinned. "Some hope."

But as he went up to the house the grin went from his face. There was a police driver sitting behind the wheel of the car.

In the big main room of the farm were the Duchess and a police inspector. He was a broad-shouldered man with a pleasant, square face with deep lines weathered into it as though time, trouble and the battering of the world's darker trials had marked it hard. He had grey hair and steady brown eyes and, Smiler thought, did not look the kind of man anyone would fool about with. He sat at the table. In front of him was a plate of biscuits and an untouched glass of the Duchess's cider.

The Duchess put a motherly hand on Smiler's shoulder and said, "Sammy, this is Police-Inspector Johnson from Bristol."

Smiler said nervously, "How do you do, sir?" and held out his hand.

The Inspector smiled and shook hands and then said, "I'm very well, thank you, Samuel Miles. Now sit down over there, lad, and we'll have a little chat."

As Smiler sat down, the Duchess said, "I'll leave you two alone."

When she was gone from the room, the Inspector gave Smiler a long, steady look, cleared his throat and said, "Well, you've led us a merry old dance, haven't you? And done it very well, I'd say, considering half the police in the country have been looking for you. With that fair hair, blue eyes, and freckles you stand out like a bright penny amongst a bunch of dull old coppers." He chuckled suddenly and added, "That's a joke, lad. Dull coppers."

Smiler said, "I know, sir, but . . ."

"But you weren't sure whether it was in order to laugh, eh?"

"Yes, sir. Am I going back to that approved school, sir?"

"Don't let's rush things, lad. There's some details and questions first. And –" the Inspector's voice hardened – "I want straight answers. Right?"

"Yes, sir."

"Good. You say this Johnny Pickering stole the old lady's handbag and tossed it to you as he ran away?"

"Yes, sir."

"He was not a friend of yours?"

"No, sir. I knew him, but he wasn't a friend. I didn't like him and he didn't like me."

"I see." The Inspector put his hand in his pocket and pulled out a piece of writing paper and put it in front of Smiler. "Have you ever seen that before?"

Smiler looked down at the paper. On it was written in capital letters: THE SANDS OF TIME ARE RUNNING OUT AND YOU KNOW WHAT YOU HAVE TO DO OR ELSE.

Smiler shook his head. "Never in my life, sir. What is it?"

"I ask the questions, lad. You give the answers. That note was sent to Johnny Pickering and quite a few others like it. You any idea who could have written them?"

"No, sir."

"Recognize the writing?"

"No, sir."

"How long is it since you saw Mr. Jimmy Jago?"

Puzzled, Smiler said, "Not for weeks and weeks, sir. No more's the Duchess."

The Inspector grinned. "I didn't ask you whether Mrs. Jago had seen him lately. Just answer the question straight. Have you ever heard of Maxie Martin?"

"No, sir. Who's he? Oh, I'm sorry, sir."

"Ever heard his name mentioned?"

"No, sir."

"Have there ever been any strangers visiting here? Someone perhaps you might have been told to forget you'd ever seen?"

"No sir,."

"You're sure?" The Inspector's voice was suddenly severe, a little frightening.

"Yes, sir. I'm sure, sir. And please, sir – what's this got to do with me giving meself up?"

The Inspector's face slowly creased into a smile, and he said, "Nothing. That's clear. Well, that's about all, I think. There's just a few small details to get settled. Until your father gets back, do you want to stay here or go back to live with your sister and her husband in Bristol?"

For a moment or two Smiler looked blankly at the Inspector. Then, puzzled, he said, "But how can I do either, sir? I've got to go back to the approved school."

"Approved school? Oh, that." The Inspector grinned and shook his head. "That won't be necessary. Somebody else is going instead. More or less volunteered to."

"Sir?"

"Johnny Pickering, lad. We went along yesterday morning early to ask him a few questions about all this. Sitting at breakfast he was. Eating eggs and bacon and reading his morning post. He had that letter in his hand." He nodded at the paper on the table. "He took one look at my men, jumped almost out of his skin with fright and made a clean breast of things——"

"Oh, no sir," Smiler almost shouted. "He couldn't have done because the pebble hasn't dropped and——"

"I don't know anything about pebbles, lad. But the penny certainly dropped for him." He stood and gave Smiler a warm smile, and then said gravely, "Samuel Miles, it is my duty to inform you that you are a free man. You were unjustly convicted and, no doubt, in due time some form of compensation will be made to you. In the meantime – where do you want to be? Here or with your sister in Bristol?"

For a moment Smiler stared at him open-mouthed, a whirl of emotion almost making him giddy. He couldn't believe it! He couldn't believe it!

"Here – take some of this. Can't stand the stuff myself." The Inspector handed Smiler the untouched glass of cider.

Like an automaton Smiler took it and drank unthinkingly, draining the glass.

The Inspector chuckled. "You're a good Devonshire cider man, I see. Perhaps you should stay here."

"Oh, yes, sir! Yes, sir – please."

"That's it, then."

"Oh, thank you very much, sir."

"Don't thank me. Thank whoever wrote this." He picked up the letter and put it in his pocket. "Now, pop off with you. I want a last word with Mrs. Jago before I go. And, Samuel Miles, remember this always. No matter what trouble you get into, rightly or wrongly, there's only one way of dealing with it. Face up to it. Don't run away from it."

"Oh, yes, sir . . . I know that now. But still . . ." Smiler paused.

"But still what?"

"Well, sir – to be honest, although it's been a worry at times I wouldn't have missed the last year for anything, because you see, sir, I would never have known about wanting to be a vet., and Fria and the Prince, and . . . Oh, gosh!"

The Inspector cocked one eyebrow at Smiler and said, "Perhaps you'd better go and lie down. All the excitement and then the cider have been a bit too much for you."

Up in his room Smiler threw himself on his bed and kicked his legs in the air and it was all he could do not to shout his joy aloud. He was out of trouble! He could stay here! He didn't have to go back to Ethel and Albert. Better still. No approved school. Completely cleared, he was. An innocent man. Gosh, that Johnny Pickering! Blimey Old Reilly, he'd like to have seen his face when the police walked in. Bet he never finished his eggs and bacon and——"

He jumped off the bed suddenly. Johnny Pickering and the pebble. He looked at the mantelshelf, at the small clay model. There was Johnny Pickering, shoulders bowed but – miraculously – the pebble was no longer on his back. It had slipped free from his shoulders and lay on the shelf at his side. Smiler stared at it in awe. Crikeys, the Duchess had been right! (Much later the thought occurred to him that maybe the Inspector had told her everything before he had been called to the farmhouse and, while he was being questioned, she had slipped up and taken the pebble off. Then he pushed it loyally from his mind. Not the Duchess. Oh, no. She would never do a thing like that.)

That evening at supper – which was a very happy affair – Smiler said to the Duchess, "Who do you think wrote all those letters to Johnny Pickering?"

"Well, who do you think?"

"I don't know. It wasn't you, was it, ma'am?"

"No. But it was a good friend of yours." The Duchess smiled, one hand stroking Scampi who sat in his usual place on her lap. "Someone, too, who travels around a bit."

Smiler cried, "Mr. Jimmy! Is that it?"

"I'd guess so, Sammy. That's the thing about Jimmy. No trouble's too much for a friend."

"Gosh, that was pretty clever of him. Sending those things and sort of preying on Johnny Pickering's mind and then when the police walked in – Whow! No wonder he blurted it all out."

"That was in Jimmy's mind all right."

Smiler was silent for a moment or two and then he said quietly, "Why was the Inspector so interested in Mr. Jimmy and all that? And he asked me, too, if I'd heard of anyone called Maxie Martin or seen any suspicious strangers around here. I didn't get that at all. Did he ask you that, ma'am?"

"More or less."

"And do you know anything about Maxie Martin?"

Pursing her lips a little, the Duchess eyed Smiler across the table and then said quietly, "Yes, I know someone called Maxie Martin. And I think it's time you did, too. He's a man who was in Princetown prison and escaped nearly two months ago. The police are still looking for him. The reason they're interested in us is that Maxie Martin is Mr. Jimmy's half-brother."

Eyes wide, Smiler said, "An escaped convict! And he's Mr. Jimmy's half-brother. . . . Oh, I see. The police must think that Mr. Jimmy helped him."

"They certainly do."

Smiler let this sink in for a moment or two, and then he said, "I suppose I'd better not ask you if he did help Maxie Martin?"

The Duchess smiled. "You're growing up, Sammy. You couldn't have put it more diplomatically. No, I don't think you'd better ask me."

"Anyway, I don't care if he did help him. He helped me, too. He must have had a good reason. What's a half-brother?"

The Duchess shook her head, her curls bobbing gently and said, "Not anything, really. It's what they liked to think they were. The Duke and I . . . well, when Jimmy was about ten years old, we more or less adopted Maxie. His mother and father were travelling people and they both got killed in an accident on the road. So we took Maxie, and he and Jimmy became like twins. Always in one another's pockets, always in mischief and so on together."

"I see. But why did Maxie go to prison?"

"Because of his wife. She was a Romany, a lovely girl, and Maxie loved her. He thought the sun rose in her eyes in the morning and the moon floated there at night. He worshipped her. But she was a wild thing and one day she ran off with another man, after telling Maxie that she didn't love him any more. Maxie had to take it, and he did. But after about a year the other man . . . well, he treated her badly, knocked her about, and eventually he left her ill and without money and . . . well, she killed herself. So Maxie went after the man and killed him."

"Crikeys!"

"There was no way the law could punish the man, so Maxie made his own law – and he went to Princetown."

"But Mr. Jimmy stood by him and helped him to escape and even now he's——"

"That's another story, Sammy, and you can tell it any way you like to yourself. So far as I'm concerned Maxie Martin was like a second son. But, as you know, the law of the land is the law. You can't go round making your own laws."

"Oh, yes, I know that, ma'am. But I can see why Mr. Jimmy . . . well, if someone's like your own flesh and blood, you've got to stand by them, haven't you?"

The Duchess got up from her chair and looked down at him. She said solemnly, "It's a good question and as old as time, but as far as I know nobody yet has ever found a true answer to it."

That night as Smiler lay in bed in the dark, he suddenly sat up with a jerk, remembering something which had long gone from his mind. Highford House and Mr. Jimmy Jago and the little hazel besom and . . . and . . .

11

∾ *The Dangerous Days* ∾

The days of May came and went, and each fresh
day put on some new brilliance and colouring to
garb itself with the high panoply of summer. The
nests held fledglings, hungry ever, gaping great
orange-skinned throats upwards for their food.
The growing young cuckoos, strangers in hedge-
sparrow and reed-bunting nests, had long hoisted
the legitimate fledglings into the hollow of their
backs and tipped them out of the nests to die.
Summer is birth and death and joy and despair.
The may trees bloomed in a cloudburst of white.
Dragon and damsel-flies nymphs climbed the river-
weed stalks to the surface and shucked their
grotesque disguises to hatch and fly winged in blue
and silver, copper and green-bronzed ephemeral
glory under the sun. Gorse and bloom misted the
meadows and river-banks with their Midas touch.
The Spring lambs had grown leggy and awkward,
forsaking the grace and joy of their young games.
The rhododendrons around Highford House made
a patchwork of red and purple against the dark
green of firs, and the white and red candles of the
chestnuts were in full blaze. It was a time of
hunting and being hunted, a time of hard labour
and danger for every creature that had young to
feed and foster. For them this was no holiday time.
Nature had opened her summer school and there

was never a second chance if a single of her lessons went unheeded.

Before June was in, Smiler paid a visit to Albert and Sister Ethel in Bristol and his sister never once grumbled at him, not even when he upset a cup of tea on the new carpet of her front parlour. He told them all his adventures and left with them a letter to be sent to his father. And he learnt that his father would soon be back home. But although he had quite enjoyed visiting them, he was happy to return to Devon.

Long before this, of course, he had written to Laura and given her all the news, and the letter which she had sent back was so private and precious that he decided that he would keep it all his life and never let anyone else see it. In the letter was a photograph of Laura which he put in a frame and it now stood on the mantelshelf in his bedroom, alongside the clay figure of Johnny Pickering, pebble at his feet, which he had not been able to bring himself to throw away because he felt that it was part of his good luck and had to be kept.

He went regularly to Mr. Samkin and one evening, when Sandra was not there, he told him all about himself and his adventures. He was the only one in the neighbourhood that he told except, of course, P.C. Grimble, who now always stopped and had a chat with him when they met.

Sandra Parsons had become more of a problem to him because she was forever hanging around or asking him to tea, or to Barnstaple to go to the cinema. It was as though she knew that he had no

227

thoughts for anyone but Laura and cheerfully and saucily took this as a challenge, enjoying his embarrassment which was considerably increased now, because whenever other people were around she would refer to him as "Sammy, my darling" – and this particularly if Trevor Green was present.

And, as often as he could, Smiler went up to Highford to visit the peregrines.

Just over four weeks after Fria's last egg had been laid the first peregrine was hatched, breaking out of its shell with the help of the rough egg-tooth on the end of its beak. Four days later there were three nestlings in the recess and Fria brooded them now, feeling their living stir beneath her body. For almost a week Fria refused to leave the eyrie, even to catch the food the tiercel would have dropped to her. The tiercel brought the food to the lip of the recess and Fria would feed there. Prince would stand by, watching her eat, and now and then they would talk to one another in harsh croakings and low whickering noises.

The first time that Smiler saw Prince bring food to the ledge he guessed that the eggs must have hatched and his hands shook as he watched the pair through his field-glasses. He decided that he would come up daily and the first time that he saw Fria and the tiercel off the eyrie together he would put up his ladder and have a look at the recess.

At Highford Maxie Martin was still living in his underground vault and was getting worried because he had not heard from Jimmy Jago and his food was beginning to run short. But until his

228

food was gone he had no intention of leaving the place. Jimmy would come. He had all the faith in the world in Jimmy. But life he knew was full of the unexpected and if, by some stroke of Fate, Jimmy did not come – then he would have to look after himself. In the meantime he took his exercise at night and before going down at first light he would stand and watch the tower and the peregrines.

He knew before Smiler that the eggs had hatched because one morning after the first egg's hatching, he picked up from the foot of the tower part of the broken shell which Fria had cleared from the recess. The following morning there was more shell on the ground. As the light crept over the hill Maxie would stand and watch the dark silhouette of the tiercel perched on the tower-top take slow colour from the sky, revealing sleek slate-dark wings and tail, the pale chest-mantle with its bold streaks and the face-markings growing plainer each moment. He waited always until the tiercel with a soft *kak-kak-kak* to his mate would launch himself into the air and start the first hunting sortie of the day. When that happened Maxie knew that it was time for him to go to ground.

Two weeks after the last peregrine was born Smiler saw the young. It was a Saturday afternoon and from the house roof he saw Fria come to the edge of the recess, shake her plumage and fly off to join the tiercel who was hanging a thousand feet up above the wood.

Smiler climbed down, got his ladder and set it

229

up inside the tower. He climbed up to the back of the recess and looked in. It was a moment he was never to forget. The three peregrines were huddled together not more than a foot from him. Their eyes were now open and their bodies were covered with a greyish-white, fluffy down. One, a falcon, larger than the others, was propped up on its bottom, its back resting against the other two, and its feet were pushed out in front to keep it in position. Three of them . . . Fria's babies . . . Smiler had a moment of intense pride. Fria had come from captivity and into the wild state which should always have been hers. She had learned to look after herself, had been joined by a mate and now had young. Although he knew that it really had little to do with him, he felt as though he had been of some help . . . that, maybe, if he hadn't been around it would never have happened.

As he balanced on the ladder watching the young there was a call from outside the tower and the three peregrines suddenly stirred into activity, thin necks raised, heads wobbling and their beaks open. A shadow darkened the outside of the recess and Fria was on the ledge holding a pigeon.

Smiler stood transfixed, hidden by the inner gloom of the tower, and for the first time in his life – though he was to see it again – he saw a falcon feed her young. She plumed the dead bird and, tearing off small scraps of flesh, held them in the edges of her beak and presented them to the young who grabbed them from her, snatching and fighting feebly for their food. Now, really close to Fria, Smiler saw the change in her, the glossiness of her plumage, the golden boldness of her cere and legs, the intense, vital light of her eyes and the imperious regality of her masked face. Fria she was, Fria free and now Fria a queen in her own domain, nobility marked in her every movement.

He wrote to Laura that night and told her all about it. His diary for that day read:

There are three peregrines. Eyases they really should be called. They're funny things. In a way like little, feeble old men. One is much bigger than the others so I think Fria must have brought off a falcon and two tiercels. She flew off after feeding them and I didn't stay to watch longer in case she spotted me.

Trevor Green came up the hill as I was coming back. He hooted and swerved his car towards me a bit. A pretty poor sort of joke I thought. He's got a mean face and I don't like him – but since I'm pretty sure now he let Fria loose in the barn I suppose I should be thankful to him.

* * *

As often as he could, Smiler got away to watch Fria and Prince. But now, with June half done, there was a lot of work on the farm. In the evenings when he was not with Mr. Samkin he worked on his own, so that except for a quick visit during the week it was usually on Saturday or Sunday that he made his real trips to Highford.

One weekend he climbed his ladder when the

parent birds were away from the eyrie. He was surprised at the change in the peregrines. Already the signs of feathering showed in their down and they were active, if not entirely steady, on their feet. While he watched, two of them fought together over the clean stripped carcase of a small bird. The other, eyes alert, pecked at the occasional fly or bluebottle that had taken up quarters in the recess to scavenge on the remains of the kills which lay on the ledge. This time, as he watched, the tiercel came to the recess with a small, collared dove. But within a few seconds of landing he must have sensed Smiler's presence or seen some slight movement he had made. He gave a sudden cry and flew off, leaving the young birds to harry and worry around the dead dove, clamouring in frustration.

It was that weekend that Trevor Green – already once the instrument of fate in Fria's life – discovered the peregrine's eyrie. On the Friday evening he asked Sandra Parsons if she would go to a dance with him in a near-by village on the following night. Sandra said that she couldn't because she was going out with somebody else. This was not the truth. She had neglected her work with Mr. Samkin recently and Mr. Samkin had made it clear that she had better do something about it. She had decided that she would work at her studies each evening over the week-end – but she was not going to tell Trevor Green that.

He said, "What are you doing then?"

"That's my business."

"Who are you going out with and where?"

"Wouldn't you like to know."

232

"I can guess. It's that Sammy Miles."

"Maybe, and then maybe not." Although basically she liked Trevor, there was an imp of mischief in her which prompted her always to tease him. One day she probably would marry him, but there was no call to let him think that he already owned her.

Sourly, Trevor Green said, "I can't see what you see in him. All those freckles and that snub nose."

"Listen to who's talking. Take a look at yourself in the mirror. You're no oil-painting. Anyway, I didn't say I was going with him. As a matter of fact –" it was fiction, and sparked in her by the glum look on Trevor's face and the exciting feeling of the power she had over him – "I'm not going out with him. It's a boy I met in Barnstaple. A doctor's son. He's tall and dark and an absolute dream – and that's all I'm going to tell you."

But Trevor Green did not believe her. He knew Sandra, knew that often she would say the first thing that came into her mind. She was going off with Sammy Miles, he was sure of that. Mooning about in the woods or talking about poetry and books.

He decided to watch the farm at Bullay brook the next evening and make sure for himself. So it was that at half-past seven when Smiler came out from an early supper and set off to pay a visit to Highford, Trevor Green was watching him from the hazel copse just above the stone bridge over the brook.

He began to follow Smiler, working up through

the fields at the side of the hill road, and he was certain in his mind that he was off to meet Sandra somewhere in the woods.

Half an hour later Trevor Green, somewhat puzzled, stood hidden in the rhododendron bushes beyond Highford House and saw Smiler climb on to the roof of the ruined building and sit down behind the parapet. He decided that this must be a secret meeting-place which Sandra and Smiler used, so he settled down to wait.

A few minutes later Trevor Green saw the tiercel. Prince came back over the woods from the north, flying high and holding a greenshank which he had taken over the first tidal stretch of the Taw miles downstream.

The tiercel stooped from a thousand feet in a steep dive, whistled down over the far flank of the wood and then flattened out twenty feet above the rough pasture at the far end of the old parkland. The bird streaked across the grassland, swung sideways in a half roll to clear the ruined house and then rose to the top of the tower. Without stopping, the tiercel – which had grown more and more cautious as the young birds grew – slid by the opening of the recess, checked momentarily, and dropped the greenshank on to the recess lip and was gone, winging out of sight down the slope to the river.

From the moment the tiercel had streaked across the parkland, Trevor Green had watched the whole maneuver. He was a countryman and, recently, he had heard rumours that some people had said they had seen a pair of peregrines around the district. He was quick-witted enough, too, to wonder if one of them could have been the falcon which he had set free in the barn. He remained where he was, watching the tower and Smiler.

Half an hour later Fria came out of the eyrie, her young fed, and launched herself into the air. She flew up lazily towards the big chestnut in the centre of the parkland. Trevor watched her rise higher and higher on quick wing-beats. When she was far up in the air, the tiercel came down from the heights above her, stooped past her playfully and called. Fria turned over and chased after him and for the next few minutes the peregrines played and wheeled, dived and stooped in the pale violet light of the thickening dusk.

Smiler watched them through his glasses, standing up on the roof in full sight of Trevor Green. And Trevor Green watched them, too. In the one was a surge of joyful delight at the heart-stopping aerobatics of the two birds, and in the other delight, too, but of a dark and revengeful kind. Wounded by Sandra's treatment of him, the farmer's son sought now only the satisfaction of wounding someone else in his turn. He moved away, back into the woods, knowing exactly what he would do. He would shoot both the birds. That would take the smile off Sammy Miles's face.

* * *

On the Sunday morning Smiler had an early breakfast and was away to Highford just as the dawn was beginning to break. He was early

235

because he had promised Mr. Samkin – who in conversation with him had learned that Smiler had only been to church about four times in his life – that he would go to church with him in the village. Smiler wasn't over keen about it, but since it would please Mr. Samkin he felt he had to do it. All those dreary hymns and things, he thought to himself as he walked along, and someone spouting away about saving your soul. . . .

On this Sunday morning, too, Trevor Green was up early and making his way by a different route to Highford. Under his arm he carried his father's twelve-bore double-barrelled shotgun. The tower was only about thirty yards away from the roof-top. It was a good bet, he felt, that the peregrines had young. He'd shoot the male bird as it came with food, first barrel, and then, second barrel, blast a shot into the recess and finish the rest off. If he knew Sammy Miles, that would break his heart. Anyway, the birds were a pest, taking partridges, pheasants and young chicks. Good riddance to bad rubbish, and if anyone asked him about it he'd just keep a straight face and say he knew nothing.

On this Sunday morning, too, Maxie Martin was more reluctant than ever to return to his vault as the dawn began to break. Four days previously Jimmy Jago had turned up, climbing down into the vault just as darkness had set in. He'd arranged for Maxie to be taken aboard a small coaster that plied between Bideford and Ireland. Maxie was to be aboard before first light on the Monday morning – no questions asked. His only risk was reaching Bideford across country during Sunday night. Tonight, thought Maxie. Tonight he would walk out into the darkness and the vault would never see him again. . . .

He lingered just inside an empty window-space of the house and looked across at the tower. The light was coming fast. There was no dawn chorus now to greet the day with song. Daybreak signalled the resumption of food finding for the young. The silhouette of the tiercel stood carved against the paling sky. Maxie watched as the light strengthened and brought the bird's plumage to life. As he did so a movement away to his right caught his eye. It was Trevor Green coming out of the side of the woods with his gun under his arm. Maxie watched him for a second or two, saw the gun, knew him to be a countryman from his clothes, and guessed it was someone out for a rabbit or pigeon for the pot. He turned away into the house and made for his vault.

Trevor Green crossed to the ruined house and climbed up on to the parapet. As he did so the tiercel saw and heard him. The bird dropped over the side of the tower and ghosted away down the hill to the river. On slow-flapping wings, a mode of flight that was awkward and cumbersome, disguising from some birds any warning signal that said peregrine, Prince flew down the river under the overhang of tall trees. The peal were in the river now, the young sea-trout which had wintered in the estuary of the Taw and the Torridge. One jumped twelve feet below the tiercel and his keen eyes marked it as it streaked away under water and lodged beneath a boulder. A dipper bobbed on a rock. Prince ignored it. He flew over and under the hanging branches, flapping along like a tired crow. Fifty yards ahead of him a stir of life at the edge of a bank of tall nettles and willow herb that overhung the river caught his eye. A mallard duck edged out into the stream followed by four ducklings. The tiercel changed from awkwardness into a flashing, steely bolt of destruction. With quick wing-beats he dropped almost to water level and closed in on the wild duck family. The duck saw him and screamed in alarm as she beat forward. Her wings and feet slapped at the water as she strove to gain height. The ducklings scattered into the bank growths as the tiercel swept over the duck, dropped a taloned leg and clutched her by the back, the long, pointed daggers of his toes needling deep into her side and reaching her heart. She was dead before he dropped to a gravel spit fifty yards farther on.

He stood on the gravel and began to pluck and plume his kill and then spent half-an-hour eating leisurely. He bathed, made his morning toilet, dressing and fussing and grooming his plumage, and finally flew off to hunt for his family. Behind him a mink slid through the water and took one of the ducklings. Before the day was out they were all to be dead.

Up at Highford House, Trevor Green was settled on the parapet, his shotgun resting in a small embrasure through which he could cover the top of the tower. He waited patiently for the return

238

of the tiercel. The old man first, he thought, and then Mum and the young ones. He watched the recess opening on the tower, and now and then caught the stir of Fria's head and neck as she brooded the young peregrines who now moved restlessly under her, hunger beginning to coil in them.

Half-an-hour later Smiler came down the old shrubbery path. He appeared around the side of the tower and began to cross to the ruined house. Trevor Green saw him at once and anger spurted in him, but he lay where he was unmoving and hidden, hoping that Smiler would not come up to the roof. But it soon became clear that that was Smiler's intention. He crossed to the house, scrambled through the window-space and reached up with his hands to begin his climb.

Trevor Green was on the point of showing himself and holding the gun on Smiler to keep him from coming up, when low over the far end of the wood he saw the tiercel coming back. All right, he thought, he'd deal with the peregrines first and then let Sammy Miles make of it what he would. He watched the tiercel slide over the edge of the wood and wing downwards towards the tower-top. In a few seconds the bird would be at the eyrie. Behind him Trevor Green could hear Smiler grunting to himself and the scrape of his boots as he started the stiff climb to the roof. Trevor Green eased his gun into position covering the recess mouth. Whether the bird landed there or swung by in a slow roll to throw in the prey he had brought did not matter. He would get him.

Whatever else he might not be, he was a good shot and had won many prizes for clay-pigeon shooting.

Smiler came on to the broad roof parapet twenty yards away from Trevor Green. He pulled himself to his feet and, as he stood gathering his breath, he saw the whole scene. To him it seemed that everything was suddenly clamped into a cold, hostile immobility, freezing all movement in himself and in the world around him.

He saw the tiercel, tree-top high, Trevor Green lying prone sighting along his gun barrel, the sun-touched lip of the recess with Fria's head just showing . . . everything frozen solid as though the whole world and all life in it would never wake to action again. A wild rage rose in him and then burst from him in an angry shout. The noise magically broke the spell of stillness. The tiercel came in leisurely to the tower-top, checked, and raised long curved wing-tips to drop on the lip and present Fria with the dead pigeon he carried. At the same moment, Smiler leapt forward and threw himself on to Trevor Green's back as the farmer's son squeezed the trigger for the first barrel.

The shot blasted into the morning air, echoing against woods and walls. But the gun barrel had been slewed sideways as Smiler landed, and the shot went wide of the tower. The tiercel flew up in panic. Fria came out of the recess, wild with alarm, and flew straight across the roof of the ruined house, seeing below her as she passed the frantic movement of Smiler and Trevor Green as they rolled and fought with one another on the

240

parapet, the gun held between them as Smiler struggled to tear it away. Fria beat up and five hundred feet above her the tiercel hung, wailing and calling, circling and waiting for her. Below him he saw, too, the fighting movement on the roof parapet. The gun roared again and the tiercel saw the two bodies separate and one fall over the inside edge of the parapet, thirty feet to the rubble- and stone-filled foundations of the house.

Circling and wailing together now, the pere- grines, hanging high above their tower eyrie, saw a figure on the roof top, gun in hand, climb rapidly down. It bent over the body which had fallen, and then turned and jumped out of the window and raced away to disappear into the woods. This was Trevor Green, scared out of his wits, lost in an emergency, giving way for the moment to the simple primitive desire to put as much distance as he could between himself and a situation which he had no idea how to handle.

Smiler lay in a trough between two piles of rubble and stones, broken woodwork and shattered pieces of glass from long-broken window-panes. His body was lying on its side and his right leg was twisted grotesquely under him. Blood streamed from a long cut down one side of his face and spurted too from the inside of his left wrist where the main artery had been slashed by a jagged piece of glass in the rubble as he landed.

For a moment or two he came out of shock and semi-unconsciousness and shouted as loud as he could, instinctively and urgently, "Help! Help!" Then in front of his eyes, the sky and the ruined walls of the old house wheeled and dipped and spun round dizzily. He lapsed into unconsciousness.

Below ground in his vault, Maxie Martin had heard first of all the sound of the two shots then, in the following silence, the call for help from Smiler. But for one simple expedient which he had resorted to he might never have heard a sound. With Summer's coming, despite the underground channels leading off the vault, it was hot and stuffy in the chamber and he had taken to wedging a piece of wood under his manhole cover, leaving a gap of an inch or two for the hot, stuffy air to escape upwards.

A few seconds later, though moving warily and alert for trouble, Maxie stood over Smiler. He recognized him at once, for Jimmy Jago on his brief visit had told him something about Smiler. Maxie, although an impulsive, emotional man, was also a practical man. He had been in more than one emergency in his life. One look at Smiler told him that his right leg was almost certainly broken, that he was unconscious and could possibly have internal injuries, but more than that – he was bleeding to death from the blood that pumped away from his cut artery.

Maxie knelt beside him, ripped off his own shirt and began tearing it in lengths. Then he found a stone to bind into the temporary tourniquet which he must make to hold the pressure point on the inside of Smiler's left elbow. He worked swiftly and urgently, but expertly, and by the time he was finished his hands, arms and bare torso were covered with blood. Easing Smiler into a more natural position but not touching his leg, he went outside and brought water in an old can from his little tank and poured it over Smiler's face.

The cold water brought Smiler slowly round. He saw a face swimming above him and heard a man's voice saying, "Don't try to move. Do you understand? Whatever you do – don't move. I'm going to get help. You understand?"

Smiler had just enough strength to nod feebly and then he drifted off into darkness.

Maxie climbed out of the house and began to run for the shrubberies. He ran as he had never run before, half naked and smeared in blood. There was no power in his mind or his body that could have stopped him. He was running for help, running from danger into danger, into the end of a dream which he had cherished for weeks in his vault. And he ran, too, because there was a virtue in him which could not be denied.

Twenty minutes later he was in Bullaybrook Farm explaining what had happened to the Duchess. She heard him out calmly and then went to the telephone and put in an emergency call for an ambulance. When she had finished she came back and stood over him.

Maxie said, "I'll go back and stay with him till they come."

The Duchess said, "No. Bob's in the yard. He will go." She reached out and put her hand on his head, and went on, "What are you going to do?"

Maxie took her hand. "What can I do? I must take my chance – you've got to tell them something. Jimmy's got it all fixed for tonight. Jimmy would lie for me. But I won't lay that on you. Tell them the truth and I'll take my chance. All I ask for is a wash and a shirt."

The Duchess said, "Sitting in the painted tent, all I saw in the crystal for you was a man running, half-naked, covered in blood. No more." She moved towards the door then turned and went on, "I'm going to tell Bob. When I get back you must be gone. You know where everything is. I don't know the justice of things. There's only One who knows that. But there's always prayers – and mine are for you."

She went to find Bob, and when she came back Maxie was gone.

12

∾ *Envoi* ∾

Smiler was taken to the hospital. His right leg and two ribs were broken. The rough tourniquet on his arm had saved his life. It was almost the end of August before he was fit to move about normally again and his father was home and living in lodgings in Barnstaple to be near him.

Smiler said nothing about Trevor Green and his attempt to shoot the peregrines which had led to his fall. He said that it had been an accident, but after a week Trevor Green found his courage, made a clean breast of the whole affair, and discovered a new self-respect.

The Duchess told the police about Maxie Martin – though not of the vault at Highford since they did not ask – and the search for him was renewed, but he still eluded them, though the Duchess learned through Jimmy that Maxie had never joined the coaster which was to have taken him to Ireland.

Mr. Samkin visited Smiler regularly in hospital and afterwards and, when he was fit enough, Smiler went on with his studies, determined to start taking his examinations the following year.

Laura came down from Scotland for a few days, and they wrote to one another regularly and they both looked forward to Christmas when Sir Alex Elphinstone had invited Smiler and his father to spend the holiday with him in his castle on the loch.

At the end of August Smiler's father went off on a two-month trip. He was a working man and could not afford to stay idle, and Smiler – after a farewell visit to the Duchess, Jimmy Jago and the peregrines, went to live with his sister Ethel and Albert in Bristol, which to his surprise he found far from unpleasant.

On his last visit to the peregrines, the young birds were flying, two tiercels and a falcon. A few local people had quietly formed a protection society to look after them. In those few hours while Smiler lingered near the tower, watching the family in the air, the young peregrines learning their flying skills from Fria and Prince, he was filled with a quiet joy at the sense of freedom and purpose that they seemed to communicate to him. He had had a tiny hand in it. Nothing could ever take that from him.

*   *   *

As autumn died the tiercel adult disappeared. The watchers, who knew the family now, guessed that he had already migrated. Soon after him went the young falcon in her juvenile plumage and then, one by one, the young tiercels.

Fria stayed for another week and would hang high in the air, circling over the tower, wailing and calling as though some urgent spirit possessed her whose commands she could not follow. She rested on the tower-top at night and during the day would hunt quickly for herself and then fly high, a speck lost against the sky, wailing and calling.

Then, on a day of roaring north wind with high-piled clouds racing in from the sea, she rose from the tower and beat swiftly up into the wind, feeling it lift her and swing her forward on its massive power. She headed due South, over Dartmoor, over the tor where Prince had once rested, and was soon high above the grey glitter of the English Channel.

But she left Prince, the tiercel, behind. For weeks now his body had lain out in the changing weather on the tower-top, hidden from sight except to the wailing Fria. He lay on his back, his legs stretched stiffly to the sky as though he had died struggling to reach it. He was a near skeleton, fly- and vermin-cleaned. Death had come to him, as it does to so many of his kind, through the slow poisons of man, spread over and leached out of the land, moving along the long chain of change in the bodies of insects, vermin, and birds, finally to reach and destroy the fierce heart and proud strength of the prince of birds.

*　　*　　*

The day that Fria went, the Duchess told Bob and Bill to take down her painted tent for the winter. But before they did so she went into it alone and sat before her crystal ball. She took the silk cover from it. She looked into it and there was no desire in her to know anything of her own kind, of Maxie or Jimmy. She held in her hands a little handkerchief that Laura had left behind her on her visit and a leather belt which Smiler had forgotten to pack.

She stared into the crystal. Slowly it cleared for her, and she saw things that would be her secret for ever, and as she watched she smiled happily and was content. Then she went out into the wild wind that had taken Fria away and her red curls swung and danced in its eddies.